ANNIE
The Brides of San Francisco 2

CYNTHIA WOOLF

DEDICATION

For Jim. I couldn't do this without you.

I love you!

CYNTHIA WOOLF

ACKNOWLEDGMENTS

To the members of my Just Write group Michele Callahan, Karen Docter and Cate Rowan. Thank you for all the time you spent brainstorming with me when you could have been writing on your own manuscripts.

To Romcon Custom Book Cover Design, thank you for a spectacular cover.

Thank you to all my spectacular fans. If you'd like to join my newsletter or learn more about me check out the links below:

WEBSITE – www.cynthiawoolf.com

NEWSLETTER - http://bit.ly/1qBWhFQ

CHAPTER 1

May 1868

Annie Markum White set her valise beside her on the porch of the huge white stone mansion. It weighed heavy in her hand after her long walk along the streets of San Francisco. Dog tired, her feet and ankles so swollen she wondered how she'd get off her half boots. She rested a moment, leaning against the side of the house, before knocking. Having endured the censoring looks, pretending she didn't care, Annie rubbed her hand over the reason for those looks, and for her long journey, her swollen belly, covered by her black gown. She was doing what she'd told herself she wouldn't do, she was asking for help.

"It's all right little one. Mama won't let anything bad happen to us, no matter what." She took a deep breath, smoothed her hair as much as possible. A hunger pang hit her, this time her back hurt as well, but she ignored it as she had done all day. She lifted the door knocker on the massive entrance to the mansion, letting it fall back to the door and then did it again. She heard the sound echo through the house.

The door opened on a butler wearing a black suit, white shirt, cravat and gloves.

"Good day, madam. How may I assist you?"

"I'm here to see Mrs. Malone."

"Who my I tell her is calling?"

"Annie White. Annie Markum White. I'm a friend of Mrs. Malone's."

"Yes, madam. Please come in."

With a nod, Annie bent to pick up her bag.

"No, madam, please. I'll get your valise."

The man stepped out, picked up her bag then led her inside.

"If you'll wait here in the foyer, I will inform Mrs. Malone of your arrival."

A few minutes after the butler disappeared, she spotted Nellie hurrying down the hall toward her. She was a little heavier and moving a little slower than Annie remembered. Her hair, still the beautiful blond color, was pulled back by combs on the sides of her head. As she came closer, Annie saw circles under Nellie's bright emerald eyes.

"Annie! How are you? Are you alone?" she called as she approached.

"Nellie." Annie's hand automatically rested atop her stomach.

"Oh my," her friend said. Coming to a halt, her eyes widened. "I can see how you are."

Annie burst into tears, much to her embarrassment.

Nellie wrapped her arms around her. "Shh, everything will be fine." She waved a hand at the butler. "James, please bring tea, some sandwiches and cookies to the parlor.

"Yes, madam. Right away."

By the time they reached the parlor, Annie had calmed down and stopped crying.

"Annie, what's wrong?"

"William died. He was in debt over his head and everything we had is gone. I have nothing except what is in the bag out in the foyer." She swallowed over a tight throat. "I need someplace to stay, Nellie."

Nellie took Annie's hand and patted it. "Of course, you'll stay here. I wouldn't have it any other way. For as long as you need or want. When is the baby due? Have you seen a doctor?"

"I'm past due now. The doctor said I was due the end of April and it's mid May, but she's dropped, I can feel that she's about to come."

"I want the doctor to look at you immediately." Nellie got up and pulled the cord by the door.

The butler appeared.

"James, send someone to Dr. Walsh. Tell him I want to see him as soon as he is available."

"Yes, madam." After a brief nod, he turned and left.

Annie's stomach rumbled and she secretly hoped her friend hadn't heard.

"How long since you've eaten?"

"Breakfast yesterday. I admit I'm famished."

"Why didn't you come to me sooner? Never mind. You're here now and everything will be fine."

The door opened and Blake Malone, tall and handsome with dark brown hair and gray eyes. He'd grown a mustache since Annie had seen him last. Following him was his partner and friend Nicholas Cartwright.

"Annie, so nice to see you. James said you were here," said Blake.

"Hello, Blake. Mr. Cartwright." She was hard-pressed not to stare at Nick Cartwright. His handsome face was the same as she remembered, the same one she dreamed about. His was the face that had kept her sane throughout her marriage.

Blake came forward, took Annie's hand in his and kissed the top. "You look beautiful. How are you?"

"You're being kind. I look like a cow."

"Nonsense," said Nick. "Blake is correct. You look lovely." He too, raised her hand, but he turned it and placed a delicate kiss on the inside of her wrist.

Annie raised an eyebrow then inhaled sharply. Shivers ran up and down her spine. There was no doubt now that her attraction to Nick Cartwright was still there, in full force, perhaps even stronger now. With her pregnancy all of her emotions seemed more intense.

"Thank you, both. You're sweet." She looked at Nick. He was still as attractive as he been at Nellie and Blake's wedding a year ago. Had it really been so long?

Nick stood there, his thick brown hair shimmering with streaks of gold, his brown eyes twinkling with what she would swear was mischief.

He cocked an eyebrow. "I'm anything but sweet, Miss Markum."

"Mrs. White, actually. I've been married since we last met, Mr. Cartwright, but I'd prefer that you call me Annie." Miss Markum reminded her of the time before her marriage, when life was easier and had seemed so boring. She couldn't regret her marriage because it had given her the gift of her baby, but still, she had dreams yet to be fulfilled.

"And I'm Nick, if you please."

"Yes, Nick," interjected Nellie. "Annie has been married *and* widowed in the past year. I've told her she can stay with us for as long as she wants."

"Of course," said Blake. "We've more than enough space and it looks like Daniel will have someone to play with very soon."

"Daniel?" said Annie.

"Our son," said Blake.

"He's just two weeks old," said Nellie. "As soon as you've rested we'll go upstairs and get you settled and you can see him, and Violet and Henry too. They'll be thrilled to see you."

That explained Nellie's weight gain and the circles under her eyes from lack of sleep. A new baby.

"I've missed you and the little ones. It seems like it was a hundred years ago that we made the trip from New York for me to marry William and you to marry Blake. William wasn't up for visiting much. I can see your marriage is a happy one. I'm glad for you."

Nellie reached up and took Blake's hand, smiling. "Yes, a very happy one."

James entered carrying a tray.

"Oh, I see you two are having tea, Nick and I should go," said Blake.

"Or we could stay," said Nick sitting in the blue floral upholstered chair across from where Annie sat on the matching settee.

Blake raised his eyebrows, "Or we could stay. Would you like tea, or coffee, Nick?"

"I'll have tea," Nick's gaze never left

Annie's face.

"Two more cups and more sandwiches please, James," directed Blake.

"Coming right up, sir."

Blake sat in the chair matching Nick's across from Nellie.

"So Annie, what happened? Nellie said you'd been widowed. I'm sorry to hear it."

"Yes, I married William White, the man I contracted with. I didn't really want to, but I had the agreement with him and he did pay for my passage out here to San Francisco." She twisted and untwisted the handkerchief in her hands. "He was quite a lot older than me and not in very good health, but I didn't expect him to have a heart attack and die before we'd been married a year."

"And you in the family way, it must have been very hard for you," said Nick.

James came in with a tray of sandwiches and two more tea cups and saucers. He put the cups down in front of each gentleman and the sandwiches with two more plates on the center of the table in front Nellie and Annie.

When James left, Annie said, "I'd be lying if I said it hasn't been difficult. I told Nellie, so you should know as well Blake, I have nothing left. William's estate was sold to cover his debts. Both he and his partner Seth Christenson, lost most everything, though Seth was much better off than William. He was able to pay off his portion without selling anything."

"Not to worry. We have plenty of room. There are at least four empty bedrooms and the Green Suite is perfect for you. You can stay as long as you like."

Annie dabbed at the tears in her eyes. "Thank you so much. Both of you. I don't know what I'd do if you weren't here."

"Now, now, don't cry Mrs. White, all will be well," said Nick, as he reached over and patted her hand.

"Annie, please." She stiffened. "I don't want to be known by William's name. If I could I'd take my name back and lose his entirely. I'm sorry. I shouldn't burden you with more of my troubles. Suffice it to say, my marriage was not a happy one." She placed her hand on her belly. "She was the only good thing to come of it."

"She?" questioned Nick. "Are you so sure it's a girl?"

"Oh yes, I'm certain." She smiled and warmth filled her, just thinking about her baby who she already loved more than her life. "I can't tell you why, but she settles down when I talk to her. I've even picked out a name. Evangeline. But I'll call her Evie."

"And if it does happen to be a boy, do you have a name picked? Will you call him after his father?" asked Nick.

"Heavens, no." She shook her head and pursed her lips. "If she turns out to be a he, I'll probably call him Blake," nodding her head toward the man in question, "after your friend here."

"I'd be honored," said Blake, his hand to his chest.

"But I'm sure it's a girl." Annie looked over at Nellie. "Do you suppose you could show me to my room? I'm very tired. I walked here and it took hours. My feet hurt so bad, I just want to put them up and rest."

"Oh, Annie, of course." Nellie stood and turned to Blake. "Her bag is in the foyer, please bring it up to the Green Suite. Let's go Annie. It's a perfectly lovely room and has a sitting room attached, that will work wonderfully for a nursery."

Annie scooted forward on the settee and then lifted her bulk using the arm rest as support. She hadn't taken five steps toward the door, when she stopped dead.

"Oh, my. Nellie! Help me." Fear clutched her muscles, as she felt the warm gush of liquid between her legs. She looked down. "I think I'm having the baby."

Nick was beside her in an instant. "Here, let me take you upstairs." He swept her into his arms and strode out of the room and toward the stairs.

Annie wrapped her arms around his neck, until a contraction hit her and she could no longer keep them there. "Oh, dear Lord, help me."

Nick didn't falter, just sped up and got her to the bedroom. Blake, ahead of them, held open the door. Nick hurried through and placed her on the bed.

"Blake, you and Nick get me some towels and hot water," directed Nellie. "I sent for the doctor already. The appointment was just to have him examine her, I didn't know it would be for a delivery…if he makes it. And send Bertha to me."

Nellie watched the men leave, then helped Annie to stand and began undoing the buttons on her dress. "We've got to get you out of these clothes."

Annie wanted to help, but another pain hit her and she had to sit on the bed, gripping the edge of the mattress. She knew now that the pain she'd been having for most of the day were contractions and felt like an idiot. What kind of woman doesn't know she's in labor?

"I don't think you'll make it until the doctor arrives. The baby may have waited to get here, but since she's decided to be born, she wants to come out. *Now*." Nellie smiled at her. "Is the pain better?"

"Yes," Annie panted, out of breath. "It's better."

"Good. Stand so we can get you undressed. I'll be fast."

And she was, Annie's dress hit the floor, followed by her chemise, crinoline and pantaloons. Nellie helped her wrap a sheet she'd pulled from the bureau drawer, around her, after which Nellie turned down the bed covers.

"Oh, excuse me," said Nick from the doorway.

Annie looked at him, squealed and pulled Nellie to stand in front of her.

"Nick, leave the towels and go please, so I can get her into bed."

"Of course. Forgive me." He turned and left.

Annie crawled beneath the covers. She relaxed against the pillows and let out a long sigh, happy to finally be off her feet.

Nick and Bertha squeezed by each other in the doorway.

"Good, you're here," Nellie said to Bertha. "I need one of my nightgowns for her. Actually bring two, both that button down the front."

Bertha turned and left the room without stopping. She was back with the garments in what seemed like a minute.

Nellie helped Annie into one and then back into bed.

"Thank you, I think all the walking finally made her decide to come out and play or maybe she knows that we're safe now."

"Either way, I'm glad she's ready to say hello," said Nellie.

Blake came in with a bucket of steaming water and set it on the floor at the end of the bed.

"Good. Now you should go take care of Nick. I'm afraid he saw Annie wrapped in a sheet and he may never have seen a pregnant woman in such a state of undress before."

"Then he got a treat." Blake waggled his eyebrows at Nellie. "Seriously, how is Annie?" He looked over at Annie, huffing and puffing on the bed, concern marring his handsome features.

"She'll be just fine, but send the doctor up immediately when he gets here."

"I will. You're in good hands now, Annie," he called over his shoulder on the way out of the room.

*****

Blake entered the library and found Nick with a brandy in his hand leaning against the side bar.

"A bit early, don't you think?" He pulled the cord next to the side bar and rang for James.

"Not in the least. Did you see her? She's…she's"

"The word you're looking for is pregnant."

"No, I mean yes, but she's beautiful. All that curly red hair falling free of her bun leaving tendrils trailing down her back. Those sapphire blue eyes. I'd forgotten how lovely she was."

Blake recognized the faraway look in

Nick's eyes. *He's got it bad.* "Well, you only met her that one time, when Nellie and I got married. I haven't seen her since then either. But you're right she is rather pretty."

"Pretty!" He looked toward the ceiling and shook his head, a wistful look in his eyes. "She's exquisite. Even pregnant."

"I didn't realize how attracted you were to our little friend." Blake sat behind the desk and motioned for Nick to take a chair in front of it.

"Since the first time I saw her at your wedding a year ago. But I knew she was getting married, so I never pursued it. But now, she's available, and I intend to have her, and marry her if she'll accept me."

"I see," said Blake, raising his brows, wondering how Nick could still feel that way after so long without seeing her.

"No, I don't think you do. I intend to marry Annie Markum White, as soon as I can convince her I'm sincere."

"Given her experience with a bad marriage, that could be difficult, if she doesn't want to marry again."

"I'll convince her. I will make her mine," said Nick. "I have to."

James entered. "You rang, sir."

"Yes, James. Bring us some coffee please and those sandwiches that the ladies didn't eat. We'll be here a while. As soon as Doctor Walsh comes, show him to the Green Suite immediately."

"Yes, sir. It will be done."

"After you've taken the doctor, please come and inform me that he's here."

"Yes, sir." He turned and left the room.

"James is wonderful. You're very lucky to have found him."

"I am," agreed Blake. "He needed work and I needed a butler."

"So do I. As a matter of fact, I have to hire a complete staff. When it was just me rambling around in that big house, a housekeeper was all I needed. But now that Annie will be living there—"

"Whoa, hold your horses there, Hoss." Blake slammed his chair forward and shook his head. "Annie isn't going anywhere. For God sakes, Nick, she's giving birth as we speak."

Nick waved his arm, "But that will be over soon and then—"

"And then, she'll need to recuperate and care for the baby. For a while. She won't be interested in anything except that baby."

Nick took a deep breath. "You're right. I'm just so excited that she's here and available. I'm ready to settle down. I'm ready to have what you and Nellie have."

"I understand your longing. Until Nellie, I never wanted to settle down with one woman, but after I saw her, I knew. I had to get her to marry me right away."

"Nellie is an honorable woman and Annie is too, or she would never have agreed to marry a man she didn't love. She upheld her contract."

James entered carrying a tray with the silver coffee service and two plates one of sandwiches and one of cookies. He set the tray on the side bar. "Would you like me to pour, sir?"

"No, thank you, James. That will be all."

The butler nodded once and left the room.

Blake got up and poured a cup of coffee for Nick.

"Do you still take it with two sugars and a spot of cream?"

"Yes, and today, with a spot of brandy as well."

Blake cocked an eyebrow but said nothing. He added the brandy and handed

Nick the coffee cup.

Nick took a large gulp of the hot, creamy liquid and felt the burn all the way down to his stomach. He didn't know if the burn was from the brandy or the heat of the coffee. Either way it was what his system needed.

"Feel better?" Blake asked with a smile.

"Yes." He took a deep breath and let it out on a sigh. "I'll feel even better when Annie agrees to be my wife."

"Don't get your hopes up," said Blake. "I've got to warn you that convincing her will be more difficult for you than it was for me. Nellie wasn't a preacher's daughter."

"Annie is a preacher's daughter?" His head began to hurt and it had nothing to do with the consumption of brandy. "We never really talked about our backgrounds at your wedding. She was Nellie's friend and I was yours, that's all. Figures. It couldn't be a simple matter of her falling in love with me, now could it?"

"'fraid not, my friend. Sorry."

Nick suddenly stood. "It doesn't matter. I will get her to fall in love with me and then to accept me for what I do for a living. Our relationship has got to work. Don't you see?

I've loved Annie since the first moment I met her. I can't lose her, not a second time."

CHAPTER 2

"Push, Annie, push" said Doctor Walsh from his position at the foot of the bed.

"I *am* pushing," she said with the last bit of air in her lungs. Then she took a deep breath.

"Okay, you've got him partway out, just one more good push and we'll have him—"

"Her," spat Annie, too tired to do anything more. Every muscle in her body ached. But if she needed to push to get her little Evie here, she would.

"Take a deep breath, girl and push for all you're worth," ordered the doctor.

Gripping tight to the rags tied to the headboard, she levered up her torso and felt the head push back her burning opening and then with a whoosh, the rest of the baby's body slid out.

"Well, I'll be danged," exclaimed the doctor. "You were right, Annie, you have a sweet little girl." He smacked the baby on the bottom and got a tiny wail from her. Then he took her, cleaned her off with the warm water from the bucket, and wrapped her in a small blanket Nellie gave him. "Here you go little one," he said to the crying baby. "Mama will soothe you." Smiling he placed the baby in Annie's waiting arms.

Delighted the ordeal was over, Annie unwrapped the sniffling infant, who put her hand in her mouth. She took Evie's hand out of her mouth, then she counted the baby's fingers and toes, touching each one.

Evie wailed again until Annie gave her hand back, which was immediately stuffed in her mouth.

Annie laughed. Already her beautiful daughter was demanding her own way.

"She's beautiful," said Nellie as she trailed a finger over the baby's damp curls. "And look, she's got your red hair. She'll probably look like you, not William."

"Thank God."

"So are you still naming her Evangeline?"

"Yes, I think so. I've been calling her Evie for more than nine months; I don't think I could get used to anything else."

"You hear that Doc? Evangeline White is the baby's name."

"No," corrected Annie, tightening her hold on her precious babe. "Evangeline Markum. I don't want anything of her fathers to taint her."

Nellie closed her eyes and nodded. "Markum it is. I'd better go let the men know the baby is here. I know they were anxious."

The doctor looked over at Annie, "I'm sorry but I must list the father's name. She'll have to be Evangeline White. You can go through the courts to change it when she's a little older, if you still don't want her to have that name."

Annie closed her eyes and nodded. "Thank you. I'll remember that." Then she looked up at Nellie. "Men?" said Annie unable to pull her gaze away from her new baby. "Is Nick still here? Why would he stay to see the baby? Why would a bachelor stay to see an infant?"

Nellie sat on the bed near Annie's feet. "I do believe Mr. Nicholas Cartwright is infatuated with you."

Annie jerked her head up. "You think so? He's only seen me twice in his life. How could he be?"

"Since the first time he saw you, he acted like he was hit by a thunderbolt. When he heard you were a mail order bride and getting married, the disappointment was hard to witness. Blake said he moped around for days."

"Really?" Her stomach did a little flip and she suddenly felt warm inside.

"Really." Nellie smiled indulgently.

"He is quite handsome, but Nellie, he runs a saloon." She frowned. "I couldn't become involved with a man who does that for a living. Please don't misunderstand me, I don't blame them for what they do, it's just the way I was raised. My father would have a heart attack if he found out I was seeing a saloon keeper."

Nellie placed her hand on Annie's leg. "Your father isn't here. He's not providing for you. You have to make your own decisions now Annie. Just know that Nick Cartwright is a good man, regardless of what he does for a living. And isn't that all we really want is a good man?"

"I can't think about that." She looked down at Evie. "All that matters to me right now is Evie."

"That is as it should be. Let's get you in a clean gown while Bertha changes the bed and removes the bloody sheets and water. After you're prepared, I'll go let them know Evie is here."

When Annie was ready, sitting up in bed and holding Evie close, Nellie left to get the men. She was back a few minutes later, Blake and Nick behind her.

"May we come in and meet your little one?" asked Blake.

"Of course, come in, come in."

"Let me see your little bundle of joy," said Blake extending his arms. "I've gotten very good at holding babies since Daniel was born."

He took Evie from Annie, tucked the infant in his arm and cooed to her.

Nick followed Blake in and stood beside the bed while Blake held Evie, a look of wonder on his face.

"So what do you think of my baby girl?" For some unknown reason, Annie wanted them all to be as enamored of her daughter as she was.

"She's beautiful," said Blake, as he gazed at the little one in his arms.

"Just like her mother," said Nick, looking not at the baby but at Annie.

Annie felt the heat rise to her cheeks, and knew her face was nearly as red as her hair. She looked up at Nick and saw he wasn't looking at Evie any longer but was staring at her, and she recognized the look on his face. Hunger. For her.

She was out of her mind to be thinking about Nick Cartwright right now. The baby was all she could think about. All that mattered was Evie.

"What does the baby need?" asked Nick.

"Everything," said Annie and Nellie together.

"I'll give you a list, Nick, you can pick something from there," said Nellie. "For right now, she can wear Daniel's clothes and I have extra blankets and diapers.

Evie started to cry and squirm.

"This is where we take our leave," said Blake to Nick. "I do believe that Evie is telling her mother she's hungry. They do that a lot."

Annie held up her arms to take the baby. She waited until the men had left before unbuttoning her nightgown and putting Evie to her breast. The little one needed a little encouragement which Annie gave her, rubbing her nipple over the baby's lips. Once Evie latched on, Annie gave an involuntary gasp.

"Feeding the baby hurts a little at the beginning," said Nellie. "But it gets easier. Daniel should be hungry by now as well. I'll get him and come back so you can see him. He's just the most beautiful baby boy ever."

Nellie left and was back a few minutes later with her son. Daniel had dark hair and gray eyes like his daddy.

Annie was so happy that Evie didn't have William's blond hair and brown eyes. No her little Evie was a miniature of herself. Thank the good Lord.

Nellie sat on the bed next to Annie and undid her blouse. Daniel needed no encouragement anymore. He knew how to find Nellie's nipple and to latch on. He was a good eater.

Annie watched him nurse.

"He must really be hungry to eat from both breasts."

"Oh he's hungry all right, but even if he's eating lightly, I always have him nurse from both breasts at each feeding. It helps keep milk flowing and doesn't allow one breast to become too full."

"There is definitely a lot to learn. I always thought having a child would be easy. It's not. It's painful." She squirmed a bit on the mattress, feeling the pull of tired muscles, and looked down at her new daughter. "But all the pain is worth it, to have this beautiful face looking up at me."

Annie's eyes filled with tears that rolled down her cheeks. She whisked them away with the back of her hand.

"I'm sorry. I shouldn't be crying."

"Of course, you should," said Nellie, rocking her body. "I cried all the time after each of my children was born, for the first few days anyway. It's just your body getting back to normal. Don't worry about it."

"Oh, Nellie," said Annie, her throat tight. "I don't know what I'd do without you."

"You'd have had this baby on the street is what. I wish you'd have contacted me when William died. We might have been able to help you."

Annie didn't raise her gaze from the baby. "He only died a month ago and I was too embarrassed. I didn't want anyone to know how much trouble William had left me in." She finally looked over at Nellie. "I haven't been thinking right for awhile. I think it was the pregnancy. She was taking all my energy."

"Well, you get some rest now." Nellie put Daniel on her diaper-covered shoulder, and patted his back until he burped.

Annie did the same with Evie, and was delighted when she burped, too. She looked up and saw Nellie smiling at her.

"Thank you for letting me stay here with you. There is so much I need to learn."

"Of course. That's what friends are for. We'll get you healthy and on your feet, then you can decide what you want to do." Nellie got up and paced the room with Daniel against her shoulder.

"That's just it. I don't know what I *can* do. Get married again, I suppose, but this time I will choose my husband. I'm marrying for love or else I won't marry again."

"Wonderful. Now we just have to get some men over here for you to meet. The only single man I know is Nick and you've already eliminated him, right?"

"Huh? Oh, yes. I suppose so. His business goes against everything I was taught to believe. 'Saloons are the work of the devil and those who work there are his minions' as my father would say."

"Annie," Nellie cocked her head to the side, surprise crossed her features. "Do you really believe Blake works for the devil?"

"No. You wouldn't have married him if you believed that, and so I can't believe it either, seeing how well he treats you, how kind he is to you. Still," she hesitated, confused by what she knew of Blake and what she'd been taught to believe. "I have a hard time reconciling how they can be good men and do what they do for a living."

"As I told a reverend of my acquaintance some time back, I believe Blake and Nick provide a service. First they don't run the girls as prostitutes. They are just dance hall girls, supposed to get the men who frequent the establishment to part with their money. Second, there are not enough women living in San Francisco. Without establishments like The Nugget, there would be more attacks on the so-called good women in general society, than there are now. You have to understand, men still outnumber women by at least twenty or thirty to one. Those numbers are going down. When Blake started the business the numbers were closer to one hundred men for every woman, soiled dove or not."

"I hadn't thought of it that way." She laid Evie across her lap and opened the blanket, still amazed at her beautiful daughter. "Still, it's something I must think about. Regardless of the reasons for the business, Father would say it's still the devil's playground."

"All I can tell you is that you have to do what is right for you. You can't let me or your father or anyone else, make decisions for you."

Annie nodded. "I know. I learned that with William, even though I would probably make the same decision simply to get my sweet Evie." Just gazing at her baby made tears well in her eyes. "She's all I care about now and I must provide for her in the best way possible."

"I couldn't agree more. In the beginning that's why I married Blake. For the children. I didn't take long to fall in love with him, but it took a long time for me to trust him enough to tell him so. I couldn't risk my heart, you see, until I was sure."

"Sure?"

"Sure he loved me back." She sat back, laying Daniel on the bed beside her. I had to have enough faith in him, even when he didn't have the same faith in me."

"I don't understand."

"Well, his ex-mistress was trying to kill me, and at first, Blake didn't believe me. He couldn't believe my word over Maddie's. She had everyone, except me, convinced she wouldn't hurt a fly. Ha!" She tossed her hair back over her shoulders. "Turned out she'd killed two men before coming here and would have killed me and then Blake if he didn't marry her like she wanted."

"Oh, Nellie," Annie recalled the story of the women who had tried to kill Nellie and she shivered at the reality of what could have been. "I read about the trial in the newspaper. I didn't put two and two together and realize it was you."

Annie looked down at Evie who slept contentedly after finishing her feeding. "She looks so peaceful. I haven't slept like that in ages."

Nellie stood up and nestled Daniel on her shoulder. "You'll be able to sleep now. I'll check in on you periodically and make sure Evie is taken care of, so you can sleep. You need to rest while you can. She won't give you many opportunities. They wake up at all hours to nurse and have their diaper changed. You'll get used to it, but this first night, you should try to sleep. I can take care of Evie."

Annie nodded. She was so very tired. Between the walk from her former home across town and giving birth, she was exhausted. Just one night. That was all she needed. Just one night. She gazed down at the babe in her arms, smiled and laid her down on the bed beside her.

"I'm afraid I'll squish her."

"You won't but if you like I'll make a temporary bed for Evie. She's still little enough that a bureau drawer makes a perfect bed."

"For now, I think I'd like that." Annie couldn't hold back a long sigh. "I'm just too tired and she's too new for me to be aware of her like I should."

"You'll get better, and you'd be surprised at how much you know that you don't think you do." Nellie laid down Daniel and busied with gathering blankets for a pad, then set the drawer on the mattress. "Now I'm tired and know you are too, so let us both get some rest. I'll have dinner brought up to you because you are *not* getting out of that bed."

"How long will I have to stay in bed?" She couldn't help feeling a bit anxious. "I have to be able to care for Evie and me. I've got to start thinking about getting a job. I can't let you and Blake take total care of me. I need to be useful."

Nellie picked up a sleeping Daniel and settled him against her shoulder. "For now and the next few months, you will let us help you. You'll concentrate on Evie and nothing else." Nellie shook her finger, "*You hear me?*"

Annie smiled. "I hear you."

*****

Six months later, November 1868

Annie picked up the baby and walked down stairs headed to the library to talk to Blake about finding a job.

She knocked on his library door. The room served as his office and where he greeted visitors and business associates alike.

"Enter."

She turned the door knob and went inside.

"Annie, how are you?" Blake rose from his chair behind the great mahogany desk.

"I'm good and you?"

"Fine. What can I do for you?" He reclaimed his seat.

She came straight to the point. No reason to dilly-dally. "I need to get a job. Where can I find one?"

"Annie," he shook his head. "You don't need a job. You know you can stay here for as long as you need."

"No, I need to provide for the baby and myself." She spread Evie's blanket on the floor and set her tummy-down upon it. The baby started kicking, raising herself up on her arms and then rocking back and forth. She'd be crawling any day now.

Blake smiled, watching the baby. "She and Daniel are growing so fast." He turned back to Annie. "So why do you think you need a job?"

Annie sat in a chair in front of Blake's desk. "I need to save for passage back to

New York."

He raised his eyebrows. "You've decided to return home?"

"Yes. It's really the only choice I have. I can't live with you and Nellie forever, even though you say I can. Soon you'll come to resent me and I don't want that to happen." She clasped her hands in her lap. "I need to pull my own weight."

"Hmm." He leaned back in his chair and rubbed his hand over his jaw. "Why don't you talk to Nick? I know the cook at The Nugget quit, decided he wanted to try his luck in the gold fields, so they need someone. You wouldn't have to worry about the rest of the business, I know your beliefs on that point, but cooking for the patrons and staff, would be all right I would think."

"I don't know…" She swallowed hard at the mention of Nick's name.

"Seriously, Annie, you wouldn't need to have any contact with the patrons. You would with the girls and the bartenders, but no one else. Well…except Nick." Blake steepled his fingers. "Is that a problem?"

"No, of course not. Why would that be a problem?"

"Oh, I don't know. Maybe because you

make yourself scarce whenever he comes around."

She jutted out her chin. "That's not true."

"Yes, it is," said a deep baritone voice emanating from the door to the hallway behind her.

"Nick," gasped Annie, turning to look at the man she had, indeed, been avoiding. "When did you come in?"

"Just now. Long enough to hear that you disappear whenever I come by. It's true Annie. The only time I see you is when Nellie has a dinner party and you can't avoid me. Even then, you've managed to not attend two of the four she's had since you arrived."

Nick looked wonderful. Her heartbeat quickened just having him in the same room.

He walked toward her, his brown three-piece suit fitting him perfectly.

He stopped at Evie's blanket.

"Well, who do we have here?" He scooped up the baby, gently rocking her above his head and talking to her. "Good day, Evie. How are you today? Hmm, Sweet Pea?"

Evie took that moment to giggle, and

then spit up all over Nick's beautiful suit.

"Oh, Nick, I'm so sorry." Annie rushed to him, grabbing the hanky in her sleeve she dabbed at the spit up. "She's never been held like that before."

He laughed. A rich, booming sound. "It's all right. She giggled. Did you hear her?"

"Yes," Annie smiled, reaching for her daughter. "She always giggles for you."

"All the sweeter for me."

He handed Evie to her mother, then took his handkerchief from his breast pocket and cleaned the spit up off his shoulder.

"There, all better," he pronounced. "No damage done."

Annie couldn't believe that he hadn't gotten angry, but instead was thrilled Evie giggled for him. She had to admit, her heart melted a little, seeing this big strong man with her most precious daughter.

"Now, what's happening?" asked Nick.

"Annie, ask him," prodded Blake.

She took a deep breath. "I'm looking for a job. Blake said you need a cook at The Nugget. Would you consider me for the position?"

"What about Evie?" Genuine concern

crossed his handsome features. "Who will care for her while you work at night?"

Annie swallowed hard. "I don't have all the arrangements made. We just started discussing it."

"We'll watch her…Nellie and I," Blake offered. "Annie can feed her before work and when she gets home. Evie sleeps through the night now."

Annie gasped, incredulous that Blake would make such a generous offer. "Have you been planning this?"

"No, but I happen to know that you can cook."

He smiled at her, daring her to deny it.

"Yes, I do cook. Simple fare but the food tastes good."

"Hmm," said Nick. "Simple fare is all we need. Something for the sailors coming in off the ships or the miners here to spend the gold they dug up by Sacramento. Often all they want to do is drink, but some just want to eat and watch the girls. You'd work supper, midnight snacks and breakfast the next morning. You'd have to have breakfast ready at six and then you could go home."

"I'll do a late supper, a midnight supper and breakfast." *I can't miss saying goodnight.* "I have to be able to put Evie down for the night. If necessary, I could come in cook for the early supper, come home and put her down and then come back, if I have access to a carriage."

"I'll send my driver for you or drive you myself," said Nick, rubbing his hands together. "When do you want to start?"

Annie didn't really want to start at all, but she needed the job and she wasn't qualified to do anything else. Besides, she was smart enough not to look a gift horse in the mouth.

She narrowed her eyes. "What's the job pay?"

Nick cocked one brow, and then looked her up and down like she was a piece of prime horseflesh. "Ten dollars a week, plus meals."

Gift horse or not, she needed to earn for her and Evie. "I'm cooking, my meals are included. Twenty dollars a week."

"Done. You make a hard bargain, Annie."

"When we're working I'll be Mrs. White. As much as I hate the name, it does come with some respectability and protection from your customers who might wander in."

"As you wish."

"I'll start tomorrow."

"Fine," said Nick. "We can get along another day on Flossie's cooking."

"Flossie?" asked Annie.

"She's the cleanup woman. You'll be working with her at night as well. She tries to keep the place tidy and usually only works midnight to six in the morning."

"Thank you, both of you, for the job. I won't let you down." Annie stepped around Nick. "See you tomorrow, Mr. Cartwright."

"No." He placed his hand on her shoulder, stopping her retreat. "I'm Nick. You may be Mrs. So and So when we're working but I'm Nick to everyone, including you. Got it?"

"Got it," Annie left the library wondering what had just happened. She felt like she'd been ambushed, but couldn't put a finger on why.

*****

"That went well," said Nick. *She almost turned me down.*

"You wanted a reason to see her more often," said Blake. "Now you have it. I knew she was chomping at the bit to start earning her own way. She doesn't like to be beholden to anyone, including us. Don't waste your time together. You may not get this chance again."

"I don't intend to. Mrs. Annie White won't know what hit her."

"With Annie you need to tread lightly."

"Yes, sir. I don't intend to be anything but gentle with her. She's too special." Nick grinned. "Did you see the look on her face when I got Evie to giggle? It was anger and happiness all at the same time. She was thrilled that it happened and angry that it had been me."

"I did. She's softening. Twelve hours a day of contact with you will make her either love you or hate you."

"I know." A shiver went up his spine. "And the thought of not succeeding scares me to death."

*****

Annie sat at the desk in her sitting room, part of the lovely set of rooms known as the Green Suite—named because the walls and the carpet were done in varying shades of green. The wall paper was a delicate green stripe with leaves on one of the stripes surrounded by pale green solids on either side. Carpeting was a clear emerald green that almost matched Nellie's eyes and the drapes and bedspread were gold and green brocade that looked almost like a tapestry.

Evie cooed contentedly in her crib, playing with her feet. Violet, Nellie's four year-old daughter had been in the room playing with Evie, but Annie sent her away, saying Evie needed to have a nap. Which was true. It was also true that Annie wanted some quiet time to write the letter she needed to send to her father.

November 15, 1868
Dear Father,

I'm writing to tell you that I am well. My husband William died seven months ago and I was left with nothing except your granddaughter. She is my life and my sole reason for living.

I have been lucky enough to be able to stay with friends until Evie, my daughter, is old enough to travel. The area where we live was not hit by the earthquake in October and we are all fine. Now that Evie's able to stay with my friend Nellie while I work, I will start saving for my trip home. The job I found pays me twenty dollars a week, which I know sounds like a lot, but here in San Francisco, those wages do not go far. At the rate I'm able to save, I can be home within twelve to eighteen months.

I'm well-aware that you are not able to help me with this expense; I only wish to inform you of my intent to return home. If there is a problem with this, please wire me and tell me 'no'. That's all you have to say in the wire so it will not be too costly. You can have it sent care of Blake Malone, 2809 Greenwich Street, San Francisco, California.

Ever your obedient daughter,
Annie

She read the letter over again and then

sanded it, put it in an envelope, sealed it with wax and addressed it to her father. She looked over at her daughter and saw her trying to roll over. At six months old, she was growing fast and learning more new things every day. She loved chewing on her fist or whatever was handy, getting to her knees in her crib and rocking back and forth.

By the time Father gets the letter Evie'll definitely be crawling and starting to pull herself up on furniture and walk. Even more, by the time I've saved enough money to get back to New York, Evie will be two, at least. Walking and talking. By that time will I want to go back? Do I even want to go back now? No, I'd rather stay here where my friends are. But what real choice do I have?

CHAPTER 3

Annie put on her plainest black dress. Not that any of the three dresses she owned was anything except black and plain. She wanted to make sure she was all business. Based on the conversation yesterday in Blake's library, she thought they had planned for her to work at The Nugget. It had been too easy. Blake and Nick were just waiting until she asked about getting a job, she knew it.

Regardless of the reason, she had a job and it paid twenty dollars a week. That was a lot of money in New York, but with the amount flowing out of the gold fields and sailors spending their salaries when they hit port, it didn't buy much in San Francisco.

Still that was more than she'd earn doing anything else. She should be grateful, and she was, but there was something niggling in the back of her mind.

She headed downstairs.

Blake was waiting.

"I thought I'd go in with you tonight. Figured you could use a friendly face on your first shift."

"I can. Thank you."

Together they walked outside and got into the carriage. The ride to the saloon wasn't very long, but Blake seemed determined to fill it with chatting.

"Are you nervous?"

Annie sat back on the plush, cushioned seat, facing Blake. "I guess you could say that. I've never cooked for anyone but family and friends before."

"You'll do fine. These men are just miners, sailors and business men, who want a meal to get them through until they go back home. They're not looking for anything fancy. Having eaten your cooking, I can say for certain they will like the fare you serve."

"Thank you. That's nice to hear."

He narrowed his gaze. "But it didn't

help with your nerves, did it?"

"No," she said with a small chuckle. "Not really."

"You're worried about being in such close proximity to Nick, aren't you?"

She looked down at her lap twisting her skirt with her hands before raising her head to look Blake in the eyes. "Does it show? You know, he's totally the wrong kind of man for me. I understand what you two do and why you do it, but I can't help the way I was brought up."

"No one is asking you to. We're just asking that you open your mind and your heart to what could be."

She gazed out the window into the clear night sky. "You don't understand." Conflicted, she wondered if she understood. She turned back to Blake, "My father would have a fit, if I were to be courted by someone like Nick. It wouldn't matter if I like him or not."

"So you *do* like Nick." He smiled indulgently.

She frowned. Panicked. Was she so transparent? "I didn't say that."

"Not in so many words, but you do like him don't you? And he dotes on Evie. I see you gazing at him when he's playing with her. There's a hunger on your face that can't be denied."

She looked out the window. The city, lit by gas lamps, twinkled as they headed down the hill toward the wharf. "I don't deny that I find him attractive and yes, I do like it when he plays with Evie. He seems genuinely enamored with her and she with him, but that doesn't mean our relationship can go any farther than that."

"He's not the devil your father would have you believe, nor am I. You know this."

"I do, yet it's not an easy thing to go totally against the way I was raised."

"I understand, but try to keep yourself open to all possibilities."

"I'm trying, Blake. I'm trying."

The carriage pulled to a stop outside The Nugget and Blake helped her down from the conveyance.

Blake told her the quickest way to reach the kitchen was by going through the saloon. She hurried along after him, practically running to keep up with his long strides and not make eye contact with any of the men sitting or standing in the main room.

Nick met them at the bar and walked

with them to the kitchen in the back of the building. It had an exit door that opened onto a high, brick-fenced courtyard. The room itself was long and skinny. Along one wall, stood a six burner stove, the icebox and sink, with counter space in between each. The other wall held dried and canned food stuffs of all kinds. In between the walls, down the center of the room was a counter for working on the meals and plating the servings.

"Thank you, for this opportunity. I don't know why you're being so nice to me."

"Because I like you, Annie. And I love Evie," said Nick. "I've watched her grow since the day she was born. I feel like she's mine, in a way."

"She's not yours, she's mine." Her protective instincts rose to the fore. "Don't forget that."

Nick raised his hands in surrender. "I'm just telling you how I feel. There's no need to go on the defensive. I know she's your child. I'm just trying to make it comfortable for you here."

Annie lowered her eyes and shook her head. "I'm sorry, Nick. I know you are and I'm very grateful to you and to Blake for this job. Truly I am."

"Good. Ready to get started? What's on the menu tonight?"

"Well, I have to see what you have in the way of meat in the icebox. Let's take a look, shall we?" She set her reticule on the counter, took off her gloves and walked over to open the icebox.

Nick followed her to the icebox and looked in over her shoulder.

Sitting front and center was a large beef roast. "Looks like we're having roast beef for midnight supper. It'll take that long to cook it. I also see some steaks in here. I'll cut them into strips and make steak fingers. Ever had them?"

"Can't say I have."

"This dish is strips of steak, breaded and fried, with a bowl of gravy to dip them in. Easy finger food. No silverware required. But if they want the full meal, then it would include mashed potatoes and I also spied some canned vegetables. Have you thought of paying the widows in the shanty town to can things for you? You could provide the produce and they'll provide the labor. Then you'd have a good supply of vegetables while helping the widows at the same time.

Evie and I would be there, too if not for Nellie and Blake. She says they are in desperate straits over there."

"I hadn't thought of it. Why don't you arrange it? I'll give you the cash for the kitchen expenses once per week. How you spend it is up to you. I'll increase it for the time being, until you can get the canning operation off the ground. Good enough?"

"Perfect. Now you and Blake…where is Blake?" She glanced around the area.

"He left when I came in. I assume he's in the office."

Annie's heart suddenly beat faster upon realizing that she and Nick were alone. Her hands started to shake. "Well, I…I need to get cooking if you're to have anything to serve for supper."

Nick came closer. "Why are you afraid to be alone with me, Annie?"

"I'm not afraid." *Liar.* Butterflies were flying circles in her stomach and she found it hard to catch her breath.

He reached out a finger and drew it down her jaw line. "You are, but for now, we'll let you believe you're not. You'll get used to me, and then we'll have to talk some more about what it is that is between you and I. Don't deny it. If there wasn't, you wouldn't go to so much trouble to avoid me."

"I don't avoid you," she insisted. *Liar. I'm terrified of being alone with him. Afraid I'll lose myself in his eyes. The color of warm brandy, they seem to see right to my soul.*

Nick chuckled. "All right. I'll leave you alone, for now. Get cooking."

"Yes, sir."

He ambled out of the kitchen and her heartbeat went back to normal. She peeled the potatoes, and started them cooking. Then Annie took the steaks out of the icebox, beat them with a mallet until tender, cut each of the steaks into long strips, breaded them using an egg wash and flour, before finally frying them in hot lard. She had a good hundred strips, when she was done. There were more steaks waiting to be cut, but these would be a good start for now. She took the roast, salted the outside of it really well and put it in the oven to cook for about two hours.

Next she mashed the potatoes and made cream gravy to go with the steak. Price wise, three strips with gravy was one dollar and twenty-five cents. She found loaves of bread and added creamed corn to round out the whole meal, including potatoes. The price was two dollars.

The steak fingers were a hit, and gone within the first hour. She cooked up the rest of the steak and those were gone in no time as well.

Nick came into the kitchen wearing a wide grin. "We've never run out of food before. Glad I got some of the first batch. They were wonderful. I'll make sure you have enough steak to do that every week."

Annie rejoiced inside. She'd been nervous for nothing.

"I'm glad the food was welcomed. Now it's time for me to take the roast out of the oven for the midnight supper. It's a big one, so it should be done medium rare to rare. I'll serve it as a full meal with the same accompaniments as the supper, if that meets with your approval."

"Of course. The kitchen is your domain. You can do whatever you like."

"After this roast there is no more meat. I'll need several chickens and three dozen eggs and—"

"Get whatever you want," Nick

interrupted her. "Just put it on The Nugget's tab down at Frank's, our butcher. I suppose you'll be ready to go home after this?"

"Yes, I want to put Evie to bed, then I'll come back and do the rest of the roast preparation and cook breakfast. I have the food for that, then you'll have to refill the stores."

"I'll have it done." He moved closer to her and when she dipped her head, he lifted it again with his knuckle. "I'm glad you're here, Annie."

Annie's heart pounded and her hands shook. Her reaction to Nick frightened her a bit, but she wasn't about to be scared off. She needed this job, more than she'd let Blake or Nick know. She had to earn her own passage back to New York. Her father would take her in and she'd be able to raise Evie.

But she questioned that course of action now more than ever. Was she just trading one problem for another? Since she'd gotten to know Blake and Nick, she realized they weren't the devil incarnate, but good men in a profitable, though questionable business. She questioned her father's teachings. Would he still provide her a home if he knew?

For the time being it didn't matter. What mattered was getting this meal on the table, so to speak and ready for those hungry sailors and miners. The roast came out a perfect medium rare. She served it with mashed potatoes, a beautiful, smooth gravy she made with the drippings of the beef, cooked carrots and tinned peaches for dessert. This meal went for three dollars. And went over very well. They ran out of food again.

Nick came in the kitchen. "I should have hired you a long time ago."

"Thank you, Nick. I'm grateful for all you've done for me." Annie, relieved to be using her skill and have someone notice, walked over to him and gave him a quick kiss on the cheek.

He stopped her from backing away by holding her waist.

"This is how it's done." He brought her body close and gave her a soul searing kiss. Slanting his mouth over hers, he sought entrance with his tongue. She granted it and he plunged in. He tasted like coffee and peaches, rich with cream. By the time he stopped kissing her they were both breathless and gasping for air.

He closed his arms around her back and she rested her head on his chest.

"That, Mrs. White, is a kiss."

"Yes," she panted. "So it is."

He let her go. She swayed a little and he caught her by the shoulders. "Are you all right?"

Regaining her composure, she replied, "Yes, I'm fine. It takes more than one little kiss to get me off-kilter."

Nick grinned. "One *little* kiss?"

"All right. One great kiss, but that's all. There can be no more."

"That's where you are wrong, Annie mine. There will be lots of kisses in our life together."

"We don't have a life together." She worried she'd given him the wrong impression with the kiss, but she couldn't regret it completely. It really was one great kiss.

"We will, you'll see. But right now I'm getting that crib and rocker for you. Then you can bring Evie in whenever you want."

As frustrated as she was with his attitude, Annie had to admit he was being exceedingly kind and her father raised her to always be thankful and polite.

"I appreciate everything you've done for me. I know you don't have to do any of this and yet you have. I thank you for that."

"You're special to me, Annie, very special."

She lowered her gaze. "I can't be. We are too different."

"I won't push you to believe in me, but I hope that you will, someday. Until then, I'll be patient."

"I wish I could get you to understand, I—"

He put two fingers over her lips. "Shh."

Frustrated at not being allowed to speak, she nonetheless nodded against his fingers. He'd won this encounter.

He smiled, turned and walked out of the kitchen.

*****

Annie opened the front door to leave for work and found herself staring into the face of Robert Atkins, Blake's banker. He wasn't much taller than Annie, only a couple of inches, but he was handsome with blond hair and blue eyes. He had his hand raised, ready to knock on the door to the mansion.

"Oh my," Annie stopped quickly lest she

run into him.

"Mrs. White, isn't it?"

"Yes, and you're Mr. Atkins."

"Yes, pleased to finally make your acquaintance."

"And I yours. I'm sorry but I'm in a hurry."

There was a discreet cough from behind her. She turned and saw James.

"James will take you to Blake. It was nice to make your acquaintance, Mr. Atkins."

Robert turned to let her pass. "And I yours, Mrs. White."

Annie slipped by the man and walked to the waiting carriage.

CHAPTER 4

January 1869

Annie had been working for at The Nugget for two months. Evie stayed with Nellie, Blake and their children. Evie seemed happiest when Nick was there. Her baby girl loved him and he her. Sometimes Annie thought Nick came by the house, just to see the baby.

Evie was crawling now and if Nick was in the room, she automatically went to him, without even being called. Her daughter loved Nick like he was her father. Maybe that was why Annie's resistance to him lessened day by day. She looked forward to seeing him, even though she knew she shouldn't.

Working all night was hard on Annie

because she was up most of the day with Evie. Nellie took the baby in the afternoons so Annie could get some rest, but the long hours and lack of sleep were beginning to show.

"You look tired tonight," said Nick as he entered The Nuggets kitchen.

"No more than usual," replied Annie. She was breading strips for the weekly steak finger dinner.

"That's my point. You're not getting enough rest. I'm changing your hours. I only want you to work dinner and midnight supper. After that, I want you to go home and get some rest. We don't have a lot of people here for breakfast anyway. Flossie can cook eggs and bacon for those who want something."

She could have kissed him. As a matter of fact, she wanted very much to kiss him but she shouldn't encourage him. Oh, Lordy it was hard. When those sensual lips of his crooked up into a smile she could easily get lost.

Annie started her new hours the next evening but Blake and Nellie had to go out and couldn't watch Evie, so she took the baby to work with her. Tonight, she was doing a roast that needed little preparation, so she could be with Evie.. The baby was restless and cried constantly if she was in the crib. The only thing that quieted her was to be held by Annie. Finally even that wasn't enough and so Annie sat in a chair and tried nursing her, which helped and Evie quieted, soothed for a short while anyway.

Annie was covered, but still embarrassed when Nick walked in with her nursing Evie.

"Oh, excuse me." He turned quickly away.

"I'm sorry. I wasn't expecting anyone," said Annie.

He turned back to her and smiled. "Don't be sorry. I've never witnessed a mother feeding her child before. I was just surprised."

She felt the telltale heat rise to her cheeks and knew she blushed. Looking down to avoid his intense gaze she saw that Evie was asleep. Annie pulled the baby off her nipple and buttoned her dress before removing the diaper that covered her. Then she put her daughter back in her bed.

Nick was right next to her, watching Evie sleep.

"She's my little angel, you know," he

said quietly.

"Mine, too, most of the time."

Evie stirred and whimpered in her sleep. Nick reached down and rubbed her little back until she settled.

Annie's heart softened, yet again. She admitted Nick had become very important to her but their philosophies were so different. Her father would say that Nick was doing the work of the devil. But how could someone so tender with her daughter be doing immoral work? She hadn't seen anything wicked about Nick or his business.

What was she going to do? She was falling in love with Mr. Nicholas Cartwright and there didn't seem to be anything she could do about it.

Nick frowned. "Did you feel how hot Evie is? I think she has a fever."

Annie reached out and ran her hand over Evie's little head. She did feel warm.

"Maybe that's why she's been so fussy. I think she's cutting her first tooth."

"You should take her home," he said briskly.

She waved her hand toward the stove. "What about dinner? It's almost done."

"Never mind that. Take Evie home and

don't come back until she's better. As a matter of fact, take at least a week and get some rest yourself. Now go."

Nick's insistence that she get some rest has her somewhat alarmed that Evie might really be sick rather than just teething

"I can't. The carriage won't be back for me until after midnight supper."

"I have my coach here. You'll go home in that. I'll go with you to make sure you're safe."

Annie shook her head and checked the items on the stove. She didn't want to leave Flossy a burned mess. "Thank you, but that's not necessary. It's enough you're loaning me your carriage."

"Nonsense. I need to talk to Blake anyway. Pack up while I ask Flossie to come in and finish supper."

"Blake may not be back from their outing yet."

"Then I'll wait. It won't be the first time I've waited for him to return."

Annie wasn't sure she wanted to be alone with Nick for the ride home, but nodded, took the extra blanket from the crib and wrapped a fussy Evie in the soft cloth.

"Shh, Sweet Pea, we'll be home soon

and I'll get a cold washrag for you to chew on. You'll feel better in no time." She realized, with a start, she used Nick's nickname for Evie almost as often as he did.

"Are you ready?" Nick strode into the kitchen wearing his overcoat.

"Yes. Let me put my coat on."

"Give Evie to me. When we get home, I'll get some of Blake's brandy and rub it on her gums. It should help with the pain."

Annie gasped. "Brandy to a baby!"

"Trust me. It will help soothe the pain she's in."

Annie reluctantly nodded. "I'll try anything to help her."

Annie grabbed her valise while Nick cuddled Evie close. They left out the back door, across the courtyard to the waiting coach. "I don't want to take her through the bar. I don't want them to know you're leaving just yet," he explained.

"Why? What difference does it make?"

He grinned. "If they know you're gone, they'll turn on me and riot. The customers love your cooking."

When they reached the carriage, Nick held Evie in one arm and used his other hand to help Annie up into the vehicle. Then he handed Evie in to her and climbed in himself.

The conveyance gave a slight lurch when it started moving, but otherwise it road very smoothly.

"A penny for your thoughts," said Nick.

"Oh, my thoughts are worth much more than a penny."

Evie cried and squirmed on Annie's lap, kicking her and trying to get down.

"I don't know what to do with her," said Annie, holding the baby a little tighter.

"Here, let me have her."

Annie lifted Evie over to Nick. The little girl immediately quieted and started playing with Nick's cravat. And he let her.

"Your tie…"

"Can be retied. She's happy. Leave her be."

When she was held by Nick, she was almost always happy. She rarely fussed with him. It was as though she knew he was her protector. Annie didn't doubt for a minute that Nick would give his life for Evie.

As the carriage made its way up and down the hills from The Nugget, where it sat on the edge of the bay, to the Malone residence on Russian Hill, Annie watched

Nick play with Evie. He was so captivated with her. Again she questioned her father's teachings. How could a man so kind to her and so loved by her daughter be the devil's minion?

When they reached the Malone's, Nick handed the baby to Annie while he got out, then he took her back and helped Annie out.

Annie held her arms out for Evie and Nick grabbed the valise with Evie's extra clothes and diapers in it. They rushed inside and Annie took Evie upstairs to her bedroom, where the crib was. Evie wailed loud enough to wake the rest of the house. It was a good thing they were out for the evening.

As they reached Annie's room, Bertha, the Malone's nanny, came out of the nursery.

"Missus Annie, is the little one all right?"

"She'll be fine Bertha, just teething."

Bertha nodded. "Not much to do for that, except a cold wash rag."

"I know. I'll get her taken care of. I hope she didn't wake the children."

"No, I was just reading to Miss Violet. I'll return to her now, if you don't need my help."

"No, thank you, we're fine."

Bertha nodded and disappeared into the nursery down the hall.

Annie went into her room and laid the baby in the crib. On top of the bureau was a basin and pitcher of water, with washcloths and towels. Annie poured some of the water into the basin, got one of the washcloths wet, rung it out thoroughly and gave it to Evie.

The baby immediately put it in her mouth and started chewing and sucking on the cool cloth. Relief washed through Annie when Evie stopped fussing.

Annie got another wet cloth and swabbed the baby with it, cooling down her little body.

Nick came into the bedroom carrying a snifter with a tiny bit of brandy in it. "Here, if you rub a little on her gums it will help ease the pain. She won't like it though. It doesn't taste good."

Annie looked at the liquid and realized that even if this was alcohol, she hated the cries of her baby more. She tilted the glass and stuck her finger into the golden brown liquid that almost matched the color of

Nick's eyes. She rubbed her finger along Evie's gums. The baby cried and Annie gave her back the cold washrag to chew on.

"I hope it helps," Annie felt Evie's diaper and found it only slightly damp but she changed her anyway, in case the baby fell asleep. "How do you know about babies? About easing their teething pain?"

Nick leaned a shoulder on the bedpost. "My little sister, Sarah, is twelve years younger than me and I remember my mother doing that for her."

"Do you have more brothers and sisters?"

"Two older brothers, Matt and Ethan. How about you? Any siblings?"

"No. Just me."

"Growing up must have been lonely."

"Sometimes." She looked up at him. "But usually there were lots of church members kids to play with, so I was never really alone. Tell me more about your sister. She was the baby I take it. No one in between you and her?"

"Yes, she's the baby and thoroughly spoiled by us. Any of us boys would do anything for her, though she's never asked."

"That sounds a little ominous. Have

there been times that you thought she should have asked for help?"

He scowled. "She could have asked before she married the low-life she did. He's wealthy, but he treats her like dirt. I don't know why she stays with him. He just uses her for his own ends."

"Isn't that what most marriages are? The man uses the woman to get what he wants." That was what she learned from her marriage. William wanted a hostess, he didn't want a wife. He was too busy and his mistress, generally gave him the attention he wanted. At least Annie assumed she did, because he didn't come to Annie very often. She wondered what her father would think of her church going husband if he knew.

"Not all marriages are like that. They don't have to be anyway. There's nothing wrong with each party getting what they need from a marriage."

Evie was settled and Annie looked up at Nick. "And what do you need from a marriage, Nick? Why haven't you married?"

He walked to the window and stared outward. "I've been just fine on my own for the last thirty-five years. I've never felt the need to marry before."

"What changed?"

"I met you. I have to admit seeing Blake and Nellie together and how happy they are has affected me. I want what they have. I want a family, a wife and children." He turned to face her. "I want you and Evie to be my family."

Tears welled in her eyes and Annie looked away from him before they fell. She'd like nothing more than to accept his offer. But there would be hell to pay. Her father definitely would not approve.

"I can't," she said. "You know I can't."

He crossed his arms over his chest. "What I know is that you won't let yourself be happy. I'm not the man your father would have you believe I am and you know it."

"You think I don't realize that?" she snapped. "You think this is easy for me?"

Nick ran his hands through his hair. "You're letting your father's beliefs color everything you see and taint what you know to be true."

"Shh. You'll wake Evie." Annie walked across the room and sat in the window seat.

Nick followed and sat beside her.

"I don't mean to be so loud, I'm just frustrated. I'm proud of how far I've come.

When Blake and I met in the gold fields, neither of us had two pennies to rub together. But we had dreams."

"Of opening a saloon?" Why couldn't they have opened a general store or a leather shop, almost anything but a saloon?

"Not precisely. We dreamed of being successful. Proving to ourselves, and our overbearing parents, that we were worth something. The Nugget was the most expedient way to do that. We were able to pay off the loan in no time and keep the business just between the two of us. There are no shareholders in The Nugget, just us. Though now we've used it as collateral for the family emporium, which Blake is calling an amusement park."

"I've heard him and Nellie talking about the endeavor. You're opening the amusement park soon aren't you?"

"Yes, in a couple of months. Then we'll trade the running of the businesses between ourselves. I'll be running a family business, so I can't be all bad."

"I never said you were all bad." *With the way you treat Evie and me, I wonder if you're bad at all.* " I never said you were bad at all, it's just my father—"

"Is thousands of miles away. Why do you still let him dictate to you?"

Annie sighed and knotted her skirt between her fingers. "It's complicated."

He stilled her hands, took one in his and wound his fingers through hers. "Uncomplicate it for me."

She looked down at their entwined fingers and then up at him. He watched her, his heart in his eyes. "I don't know how. My father…"

"Is not here. This is just between you and me. I want to court you, Annie. I want you to get to know the real me, not the man who sells liquor to thirsty men, but the man who cares for you and Evie. The man who can make you happy for all our years together."

"I can't. I've agreed to let someone else court me."

Nick let go of her hand and stood, towering over her like an avenging angel.

She drew backward.

"Who?" She saw the change in his demeanor. Jealousy? Anger, perhaps?

"His name is Robert Atkins, your banker. I met him a few times when he came to see Blake. He asked if he could court me and I agreed." Guilt stabbed through her. Annie knew Nick thought he was in love with her and she loved his attention to Evie. Her daughter loved Nick, too there was no denying that. She should have told him before.

He calmed before saying, "Let me court you, too. After all, I'm half respectable with owning half of the amusement park."

Annie sighed and shook her head. "Why do you insist on doing this? You know nothing can come of it."

"I care for you. When are you going to get that through your pretty head? I want to court you both. Evie is as much a part of this as you are. You want what's best for her, right?"

She lifted her chin. "Of course. That's all I want."

"Good then, I'll begin by taking you home every night after work. That will give us some time together. But I also want to be able to take you out on one of your days off. Go to dinner, perhaps the theater. Wouldn't you like that?"

She nodded. "Of course, I would, but I don't want to leave Evie with Blake and Nellie every night of the week."

"Then we'll do things we can do with Evie. I'll pick you up on Monday and we'll go on a picnic with Evie. I'll bet Mr. Akins hasn't suggested taking Evie on your outings together."

"No, he hasn't, but Sunday evening is our first outing. He's coming here for dinner."

"I see. So Blake and Nellie approve of this courtship?"

"They don't know he's asked to court me, but I imagine they suspected it, when I asked if he could join us for Sunday dinner."

"Well, what do you say? May I court you, too?"

Pleased with his persistence, she's also irritated with herself. She shouldn't want him to court her, but illogically, she finds she does. She enjoys spending time with Nick and there's a niggling little bit of hope in the back of her mind. "Very well. Yes. You may court me."

CHAPTER 5

A couple of weeks had passed and Annie was being courted by both Robert and Nick. She had to admit she enjoyed it, and found herself thinking about both of them when she was at work.

Annie heard the ruckus from the kitchen and looked out the door.

"Nick. Nick Cartwright. Nick." A woman yelled over and over again. The music stopped and several of the girls tried to calm the young woman but she was having none of it.

Annie went out and approached her. The girl had already shaken off Sally Jo when she tried to help her, but Annie had to try. The poor thing was obviously very distraught and perhaps in trouble. Her dirty blond hair hung lank over her shoulder and she had a black eye that even Annie could see from her perch in the kitchen doorway. She had to get the woman out of the bar and walked out to help her.

"Miss, can I help you? Nick isn't here right now." Annie spoke softly and tried not to upset the woman more than she was. "Why don't you come with me and wait for him?"

The woman's face was bruised in addition to the black eye. The snatches of dress Annie saw underneath her black wool coat were torn and well worn before that. She knew the signs of abuse from working with the women in her father's flock.

"Come on honey, let me make you a cup of tea and we'll wait. Nick always comes to the kitchen before he goes up to the office, so you'll see him there first."

The woman stopped yelling, eyed Annie and asked, "Why would he go to the kitchen?"

Annie had her talking, now if she could just get her out of the bar. "He loves to play with my baby. Why don't you come meet her? I have Evie with me tonight."

Her eyes widened and she whispered, "You have a baby?"

"Yes, come meet her."

Annie wrapped her arm around the woman's shoulders. They seemed to be about the same age, but Annie felt older as one who comforts others always does. It was something she'd learned from an early age.

The girl was shorter than Annie's own five-foot-eight height, by several inches, and she felt the girl's bones under the arm she had wrapped around her.

The woman went with her, and the music started up again in the main room. Annie was the only woman who was dressed normally. The dance hall girls were wearing their provocative costumes, but Annie seemed approachable. That's the only thing she could think of as to why the woman agreed.

Annie tried to keep her talking. "What's your name, hon?"

"Sarah. Sarah Roland."

"Oh, you're Nick's sister aren't you?"

"Yes, how did you know?"

They reached the kitchen and Annie sat Sarah in the rocking chair next to the crib. Evie was crying because she'd been left alone but now that Annie was back, she sniffled a little and was all smiles again. She really was the happiest baby Annie had ever seen. She was so incredibly blessed.

"Nick has talked about you. Specifically when you were teething as a baby."

Sarah cocked her head and narrowed her blue eyes.

"Evie's been cutting her first teeth and having a rough time, poor little thing. Nick helped me by recalling what your mother used to do with you and the remedy worked. She's had an easier time lately. Now, next to you, standing in her crib, is my eight-month old daughter, Evie."

Annie picked up Evie and introduced the baby to Sarah.

"You're such a good girl. Yes, you are," She rubbed her nose back and forth in the chubby folds of Evie's neck. "Mama's sorry she left you alone for a minute, but now you're going to meet Sarah. Sarah, this is Evie. Would you like to hold her? She loves to be held. I'll make you a cup of tea and we'll wait for Nick. He should be here any time."

"Who should be here?" asked a masculine voice from behind Annie.

His voice sent shivers up her spine like it always did. She loved to hear the deep rumble when he spoke.

"Nick, you have a visitor."

Annie moved aside so Nick could see Sarah, holding Evie.

"Sarah? Is that you?"

"Hi, big brother." Sarah, suddenly shy, hid her face in Evie's neck.

"What's wrong? Look at me." Nick approached Sarah.

The closer he got, Annie could see his anger rise. He saw Sarah's face and her black eye and by the time he reached her the veins were standing out in his forehead.

"Did he do this to you?"

"He didn't mean to. John just got drunk and wasn't happy when I told him I was expecting."

"You're with child and he did this to you?" Nick fairly shouted.

Annie placed her hand on Nick's arm, his muscles tight with anger, his hands forming a fist.

He snapped his gaze to her.

She shook her head and said, "Gently, Nick. She's been through enough."

He gave her a curt nod. "Sarah, where is

John?" he asked softly.

Annie took Evie from Sarah and bounced her on her hip.

"I don't know." Fat tears rolled down Sarah's cheeks. She pulled on Nick's arm. "Let me stay with you for awhile. Please don't hurt him. I need to decide what I want to do."

"Of course, you can stay with me." He wrapped her in his arms, patting her back. "For as long as you want. I just wish I could have kept you safe."

She pulled back and looked up at him. "You tried. Matt tried. Ethan tried. But I wouldn't listen to what any of you had to say. I thought I was the only one who knew what to do. I had to marry John. Maybe because he was so wrong for me in all of your eyes."

Annie admired Nick even more, seeing his protectiveness toward his sister. "You should take Sarah home and get her settled."

He kept his arms around his sister but turned and faced Annie. "What about you and Evie?"

"We'll be fine." *I need to rely on myself and stop relying on Nick's intent to stick close to me. It's not fair to him.*

"No, you'll come with us. Sarah could use a woman to help her settle in. I'll watch Evie. Right, Sarah? Afterward, I'll take you and Evie home."

Sarah looked over at Annie holding Evie. "If you wouldn't mind, I would appreciate your company."

Annie looked at Sarah and couldn't turn the poor woman down. She'd been through enough for one night. "Of course. Let me gather up our things." She handed Evie to Nick. "Hold her for me, please."

"Sure. Come here, Sweet Pea." Nick held his arms out to the baby, who smiled and laughed, and swung her arms up and down in delight.

"I'll never understand why she loves you so much." Annie shook her head and pulled the blankets out of the crib.

"Because she knows I love her. She's a smart girl. Yes, you are," he cooed to the babe. "You're Nick's girl, aren't you, Sweet Pea?"

Evie gurgled and blew bubbles for him.

He laughed and tucked her into his arm. "Are we ready ladies? Let's get all my girls home and safe."

Nick handed Evie to her mother. Then

he took both her valise and Sarah's bag and led the way to the carriage. He handed the bags to his driver, and then held the baby while he helped her mother and his sister into the carriage. Within moments they were seated and on their way.

"Sarah, tell me a little about yourself. You said you're expecting. When are you due?" asked Annie.

"In about five months. I knew John wouldn't be too happy to begin with but I thought once he got used to the idea, he might like being a father. I was wrong. He was so angry, said it was my fault and how could I let this happen? I never thought he'd do this." She dabbed at her eyes with the handkerchief she'd been twisting with her fingers.

Annie glanced at Nick. The muscle in his jaw jerked as he clinched his teeth. She knew he was doing his best not to yell at his little sister.

"You'll be safe with Nick, don't you worry about at thing."

"Does she always come to work with you?" Sarah stared at Evie who bounced on her mother's lap.

"No, actually, she doesn't come very

often at all. But Nick was nice enough to get a crib for me in case I do have to bring her. The friends I live with had to go out tonight and they have three children of their own that their nanny has to watch. I don't like asking her to take care of Evie, too."

"You said Nick always comes to the kitchen first to see the baby. It sounded like you always bring her, that I'd find him there before his office."

Annie's cheeks burned. "He does come to the kitchen to see if I've brought Evie."

Sarah looked between Annie and Nick, then down at her lap. "Oh, I see."

"No, the situation is not what you think," said Annie. "Nick is courting me."

Sarah's head snapped up. "Courting you? Nick?"

"Why do you sound so surprised?" he grumbled.

"Because you said you'd never get married. Of course, that was years ago, but still...I didn't think you'd changed your mind."

"Well, I have. Now if I could just get someone to change *her* mind." He looked pointedly at Annie.

Annie ignored him. She'd been through

this with him too many times. They were wrong for each other. She shouldn't let him court her, but she had to admit, she enjoyed being with him and Evie loved him so much. She wondered what her baby girl knew that she didn't.

Evie held out her arms toward Nick.

He took her and she immediately grabbed for his tie and started chewing on the end.

"All of my ties are starting to look frayed on the ends."

Annie shook her head. "You don't have to let her do it, you know."

"She likes it. It makes her happy."

Sarah laughed. "I never thought I'd see my big brother holding a baby, much less letting her eat his tie."

"Don't pay any attention to them, Evie." Nick talked to the baby like she understood him. "You just do what you want to."

"He spoils her incessantly. I don't know what I'll do when she gets older and doesn't get her way. She will be difficult to live with, to say the least."

"Do you two always fight with each other?" asked Sarah, her gaze flitting between them.

"What makes you think we're fighting?" asked Nick.

"Well, she's not agreeing with what you're saying."

"Sarah, just because we don't agree, doesn't mean we're fighting." Annie took the tie from Evie and tucked it back in Nick's vest. "Is that the kind of marriage you had? Did you always have to agree with your husband?"

"Oh, yes, or John got very angry. He's never beaten me like this before though."

"That's not how marriages work." Annie gently patted Sarah's hand. "Husbands are not allowed to hit their wives for any reason."

"Real men, don't hit women," growled Nick. He pulled his tie back out and gave it to Evie who was starting to fuss.

She grabbed it and immediately stuffed it back in her mouth.

Sarah looked out the carriage window. "I'm beginning to realize that."

"It's about time," said Nick. "Are you sure the baby is all right?"

"I think so. He didn't hit me in the stomach." She added under her breath, "this time."

The carriage came to a halt in front of Nick's house. Lights glowed through the curtains in a couple of the downstairs windows.

With quick moves they climbed down from the carriage, and headed toward the house.

"I need to change her. Where do you want me to do that?"

"I'm taking Sarah to the bedroom next to mine. You can change the baby in there while we get Sarah settled."

"I'll follow you. You do know this is all highly improper? I shouldn't be here in your house without a chaperone." Annie shifted Evie to her other hip. The baby was squirming, reaching for Nick.

He grinned. "Sarah and Evie are our chaperones. They're all we need."

"I suppose that's true. Well Sarah anyway. Evie doesn't make a very good chaperone. She'll do anything for you."

He laughed and chucked Evie under the chin with his knuckle. "That's my girl."

Annie shook her head and rolled her eyes. Then she went into the bedroom that would have been the mistress's suite. The rooms were beautiful, done in shades of pink and mauve. The furniture was a rich, cherry wood and included the bed, bureau, nightstands and a writing desk. Draperies of mauve damask hung from the windows and two Queen Anne chairs sat in front of the fireplace, with a tall, narrow cherry table between them.

Feeding her curiosity she went through the other door in the room. It led to the dressing room, which was separate and huge. There were rods for hanging clothes, built-in drawers for underpinnings, racks for shoes, shelves for hats—everything a woman could want in a closet.

Nick put the valise on the bed.

Annie came back from the dressing room and laid Evie on the bed. Then she opened the valise and got out a clean diaper.

Quick as a bunny, Evie turned over and crawled toward the edge bed.

With a gasp, Annie lunged and caught her before she crawled off the side. It happened two more times before she gave up and put the baby on the floor until she was ready to change her. Once she got a wash cloth from the bureau and wet it with the water in the pitcher, she came back to the bed. She reached down for Evie and discovered the little one had crawled under the bed.

"Evie, come back here. Evie!" She got down on all fours and reached for her giggling daughter. "Gotcha." She snagged at the heel of Evie's shoe. It slipped through her fingers. "Come back here."

The baby crawled faster and reached the other side of the bed before Annie could stand and get around to it.

"Whoa, Sweet Pea," said Nick. "Where do you think you're going?"

Annie rose in time to see Nick scoop Evie into his arms.

"You ornery little thing, come here," She gathered her laughing daughter into her arms. "Let's get you changed, *then* you can crawl wherever you want. Yes, Uncle Nick can chase you and keep you out of trouble."

"Why aren't you two married?" asked Sarah out of the blue, as she sat on one of the chairs by the fireplace. "It's obvious you're made for each other and you both love Evie. If I didn't know better, I'd have said she was Nick's daughter."

"Our relationship is complicated," said Annie.

"It's not complicated," countered Nick.

"She won't say yes. But I intend to keep trying until she does."

Annie sighed. It was the long-standing problem between them. "I keep trying to explain to you. I can't. My father would never approve and I, well I was taught that saloons and the people who run them are evil."

"That's your father talking," said Nick. "Have you heard back from him yet?"

"No, but he may not have gotten the letter yet." She finished changing Evie's diaper, which was just wet and put her back on the floor.

The baby immediately crawled to Nick, who bent and picked her up.

"She always comes to you."

"Of course, she knows I adore her."

"Hmpft," said Annie. She wrapped the diaper in a waterproof oilcloth and put it in her valise before washing her hands.

"Sarah, do you have your nightclothes with you?" asked Nick.

"Nicholas, you do not ask a lady about her nightclothes," admonished Annie.

Sarah nodded. "It's all right. He's my brother,"

"See, she doesn't mind. Now, do you?"

he looked back at Sarah.

"Yes, I brought night things with me. I wasn't sure what was going to happen, I just knew I wasn't going back home."

"Good, I want you to take a bath. And Annie, I'd like you to help her, if you don't mind."

"Of course, where is your bathroom? Do you have running water like Blake and Nellie?"

"Yes, Blake and I were the first ones to install, both hot and cold water, in the house. Some of the more prominent members of our city are having the plumbing installed now, but it's still few and far between." He pointed to the door to the dressing room. "It's through there."

"Good. Sarah, you come with me." She helped Sarah to stand. "Nick, you keep an eye on Evie and don't let her out of your sight."

"Yes, ma'am." He looked down at Evie, who was pulling on his tie. "We'll have a good time while Mama is gone, won't we, Sweet Pea?"

Annie shook her head. She knew he loved Evie so much, it wasn't fair to either of them for her to keep letting Nick court her, but she had to admit, she did enjoy his attention. Their outings were always the highlight of her week.

She saw him almost daily at work, but that was different, their interactions were rushed. She was cooking and he only looked in to see if she brought Evie…or so he said. He never stayed long, but always came back when the food was prepared and ate his dinner in the kitchen with Annie.

When they went out, his attention was different. He concentrated on her and the baby, not on work. They would go on picnics, or just for a drive in the country. He'd take them to one of the various bay restaurants for lunch and then stay at the house and play whist with Nellie and Blake.

Annie struggled not to compare Robert Atkins to Nick. Robert was a handsome man, in a respectable profession, but there was something missing. First, he didn't want to take Evie with them anywhere. He escorted Annie, to the opera and to several balls, they went to dinner, but he never asked to stay in, or take Evie to the park.

She knew after their first few outings that Robert was not the one. Any man who wouldn't accept Evie was not the man for her.

Inside the bathroom, Annie put her mind back to Sarah. "Let's get you cleaned up."

Sarah took off her coat.

Annie gasped. The entire front of Sarah's dress was ripped open and one sleeve was completely free from the shoulder, Annie could see the threads that had been holding it together. Sarah had bruises on her chest and arms—some new and violent purple, others green and yellow, almost faded away.

"Oh, my God, Sarah. You poor girl. Come on now, let me help you."

Annie unbuttoned Sarah's dress and slipped it off to the floor. She did the same with her chemise and pantaloons. Sarah didn't wear a crinoline or petticoats. Annie wasn't surprised. Only women of means wore all that under their dresses. Most women, from the working class, wore only stockings, a chemise that hit the knees and bloomers. Corsets and crinolines would not allow them to move enough to work.

Sarah just stood there with her arms at her sides like a statue.

Annie was thankful her own marriage, though not a good one, hadn't been violent.

She was grateful not to have suffered in the way that Sarah had.

Sarah got into the tub and Annie handed her a washcloth and some soap. There were two bars. She sniffed each one. The first was sandalwood. Definitely Nicks. She loved that scent on him. The second bar was rose-scented. Why would Nick have rose scented soap? It was her favorite scent. Was he planning ahead?

Annie took the washcloth from Sarah who sat still in the bath. "Let me help you. Then we'll get you in a nightgown and into bed. Are you hungry? I can fix you something to eat."

She finished washing Sarah's pale-skinned body. She was so thin, Annie saw her ribs sticking out. "Why don't you relax and soak a little while I get you that food."

Sarah nodded. "I am hungry. I haven't had anything to eat today."

"I'll do that right now." *This is what I'm good at, preparing food and feeding people, providing comfort.* "The food will be waiting for you when you get out of the tub."

"Thank you, Annie. For being so kind to me. I don't deserve it."

"Hush now." Annie set her hands on her hips. "Don't let me hear any more of that nonsense. That's your husband talking, not you. Of course you deserve kindness, and goodness and love. Your husband does not love you. If he did, he would not treat you this way. You need to understand that. Do you?"

"I think so. That's why I left. I was afraid he'd kill me."

Annie was saddened by the pain Sarah had had to endure, but she was glad she'd left in time. "I'm sorry but you're probably right. It's good you got out when you could. Let me tell you a story. I have a friend. She was married for a long time to a man who beat her whenever they had sex. When the man died, my friend realized she was finally free. That he hadn't loved her as he professed to, because if he had she would never have been put through all of that pain. It took her marrying a good man, a man who loves her passionately, for her to realize that."

"Is your friend happy now?" There was a hopeful note in Sarah's voice.

Annie tried very hard to ignore all the damage she saw from the previous beatings this girl had endured. "Ecstatically. She has a baby who is just about Evie's age."

"Do you think I can find that kind of happiness?"

"I'm sure of it. The other thing I'm sure about is that you need to protect your baby as well as yourself." Her stomach churning she said, "If you go back to your husband, your baby is going to die. You realize that don't you. If he doesn't kill you outright, he'll beat you until you lose the baby."

Covering her face with her hands, Sarah started to cry. "I know. That's the real reason I left. The baby. If it had been just me, I would have stayed, like I always did."

Annie gave her back the washcloth, "You finish your bath now. Think about what I said and what you want. Nick will protect you. Your husband cannot hurt you here. Remember, Nick loves you."

Sarah nodded. "I know."

"I'll go and fix you that food." Annie stood. "I'll be back in a little while, you soak a bit and wash your hair. Once you're clean, you'll be on your way to feeling better."

"I'll be fine. Thank you for making me the meal. I need it, for the baby." She put her hand over her belly and rubbed it in circles.

Smiling, Annie turned and left the room. She immediately went next door to Nick's bedroom. He was sitting in a chair in front of the fire, talking to Evie in a quiet voice.

"What are we going to do, Sweet Pea? We have to convince your mama to marry me. We're a family, whether she knows it or not. We belong together. I wish she'd hear back from her father. Maybe that would help her to follow her heart. I know she loves me, her head just won't let her heart lead the way."

Annie put her hand to her mouth and bit her knuckles, to keep from making any noise. She turned and left the room, tears in her eyes.

How could she keep doing this to them all? She had to break it off with Nick. Knowing she couldn't marry him, seeing him every day and most evenings, wasn't fair to him or to Evie. But how could she take him from Evie? He loved her so much. She'd have to let him see the baby, without Annie being there, just like he was doing now when she went out with Robert.

How could God bring someone so

perfect for her, someone who loved her and who she loved, into her life, knowing she couldn't marry him? Would he really do that? She couldn't believe that the God she knew would but how did she reconcile that with what she'd been raised to believe?

CHAPTER 6

Robert came by for his regular Saturday night dinner engagement.

James announced that Mr. Atkins was waiting for Annie in the foyer.

Annie smoothed her hair and checked her reflection in the full length mirror in the corner next to her dressing table. She looked fine, better than fine. Her dress was the perfect shade of sapphire blue to match her eyes. She'd had Nellie's modiste make the garment for her. She should be in mourning but she thought it hypocritical to wear mourning for someone she didn't mourn. Besides, Annie needed new dresses if she was to attend the opera and balls and other galas with anyone, Robert, Nick or Blake and Nellie.

She'd put her up hair, holding it in place with two sapphire combs. The combs, a necklace and earbobs were the only things besides Evie that she had left from her marriage. She'd hidden them from the creditors. She refused to let them be taken to pay William's debts, as they were the only nice things he'd ever given her.

She pinched her cheeks and smiled, then took a deep breath. "Here you go, girl."

Annie descended the stairs to the foyer where Robert was already waiting.

"I'm glad you're early," she said, "I'd like to discuss something. Will you follow me to the library, please?" She was going to insist if he still wanted to see her, he must start including Evie in his plans.

"Certainly, my dear."

He looked quite dapper in his black suit and tie. His hair was slicked back with oil and his mustache waxed.

They walked into the library. Annie let Robert pass before closing the door.

"May I say you look absolutely lovely tonight, m'dear."

Annie took a breath, "Thank you, Robert." She sat on the settee and pointed at the chairs across the way. "Please have a seat."

Robert sat on the settee, right next to Annie.

She leaned away. "Robert?"

"I knew you couldn't wait any more than I could to get to know each other more intimately." He grabbed her shoulders and pulled her toward him.

"No." Fear roiled her stomach. "Robert, that's—"

"Come now Annie, I've been courting you for months. You've got to be as frustrated as I am." He leaned forward and pursed his lips.

Annie turned her head just in time and he only grazed her cheek.

"Robert, let me go."

"Now, Annie, you want this as much as I do, I know you do."

He pulled her closer, his hand slipped down her shoulder to the top of the sleeve of her dress. He latched on to the material like it was an anchor. He pulled her to him again.

She heard the rip of the fabric and gasped.

"No, Robert. No!"

She hit him on the chest as much as her

hands trapped between them could.

"No—"

His lips found hers and he forced his tongue into her mouth.

Blood pounding in her ears, she fought him, pushing, turning her head trying to dislodge his tongue.

Then he was gone.

Annie looked up in time to see him fly across the room. Nick stood there like an avenging angel. Tall, dark, his handsome features wrought with fury. She'd never seen him like this.

"What's the matter with you man? She wants it," said Robert, waving a hand in her direction. "She's just a cook at your saloon. I'm the best thing that's ever going to happen to her."

On shaking legs, Annie stood, holding the shoulder and bodice of her dress closed.

Nick started toward Robert, rage distorting his features.

"Nick! Nick! No!"

His head snapped around and he looked at her.

She saw the anger building as he glanced over her, taking in her torn dress and the bruises starting to form on her shoulders where Robert had grabbed her.

"No, Nick, please, don't hurt him."

He stood, fists at his sides and nodded curtly. "You'd better get out while you can, Robert, and don't ever come back here."

"That includes for our business. We'll find another banker," said Blake from the doorway. "One who doesn't abuse women."

Robert face, mottled red with rage and what Annie hoped was embarrassment, ran from the room.

Nick was immediately at Annie's side. "Are you all right? Did he hurt you?"

After taking a deep breath, she forced a smile. "I'm fine, thanks to you. What are you doing here?"

He took the ripped shoulder of her dress and laid it on her arm, covering the finger marks Robert left.

"You're not fine. You have bruises where that bastard grabbed you."

She lifted his face so he gazed at her not at her torn dress. "Nick, thank you. I don't know why you're here, but I'm grateful that you are."

He smiled and touched his fingers to her face. "I came to play with Evie, while you were out with him for the evening."

"He always does," said Blake from behind Nick. "Whenever you went out with Robert, Nick came over to see Evie. I think she's one of his favorite girls."

Annie cupped his cheek. "You do that for her? You really do love her don't you?"

"With almost all my heart. But there's another special girl in my heart, who I'd love to marry if she'd say yes," he said with a smile.

"Now's not the time to be asking me. I know that you just saved me from disgrace, but if I said yes now, you'd always wonder if it was just because you saved me, and I'd wonder the same thing."

Nick leaned down and rested his forehead against hers. "I know, which is why I'm not asking. Not right now." Without moving, he said to Blake, "Would you get Nellie to come help Annie? She needs another woman here to help her through this."

"Don't be silly, I'm fine." She lifted her chin and took a deep breath. "I just need to change, then we can all play cards or something."

Nick closed his eyes and let out a small sigh. "Just go with Nellie and then let's see how you feel."

She raised her head and kissed him on the cheek. "Thank you for being my knight in shining armor."

"Anytime, Annie mine. Anytime."

For several moments they stood in each other's arms. Annie felt so safe. She always felt safe with Nick. And she knew he would protect Evie with his life if necessary. Why did her father have to be a man of God? Why did he have to believe Nick did the devils work? She knew better yet she couldn't get over the knowledge her father would disown her if she married Nick.

Nellie rushed into the room. "Annie? Are you all right?"

Nick and Annie broke apart, but he kept his arm around her shoulders and her body close to his side.

"I'm fine." Annie moved away from Nick and walked toward Nellie. "I just need to change, and then we can all play cards or something," she repeated, needing to convince herself as much as everyone else.

The closer she got to Nellie and the farther away from Nick, the more her fear grew. Her eyes glossed over with tears. She blinked and felt them trickle down her cheeks.

"Nellie." She ran to her friends arms.

"Oh, honey. It's all right." Nellie put her arms around Annie. "Come with me. It's all right."

"He was going...Nick saved me."

Annie turned around and looked at Nick.

He clenched and un-clenched his hands. The rage still coursed through him.

She couldn't hold his gaze, horrified he had witnessed her humiliation.

"Let's get you upstairs and into a hot bath. You'll feel better and this will all be behind you."

Annie nodded and leaned into Nellie's side.

Once they got to Annie's bedroom, Nellie helped her out of her dress.

"This will be easily fixed," said Nellie, holding up the beautiful blue gown.

"I don't want it. I don't ever want to see that dress again."

Nellie's eyes rounded. "But Annie, you love this dress."

"No more." She wrapped her arms around herself. "Every time I see it I'll remember. Remember what happened and what's more, remember what could have happened if not for Nick."

"Nick loves you, Annie. He will always be there for you."

"No, can't you see?" She wiped her eyes with the backs of her hands. "I can't ever be with him. He knows. He knows what I am. This wouldn't have happened if I wasn't a loose woman. It's my fault. I should still be in mourning. I—"

Nellie shook her by the shoulders. "Stop it. Annie don't let Robert do this to you. None of this is your fault. It's his. You have done nothing wrong. You are not a loose woman. Nick loves you. He's always loved you since before you married William."

"He doesn't know me," Annie collapsed on the bed. "How can he love me?"

"I don't know. Why don't you tell me how you can love him?"

A gasped escaped. "I don't. I…"

"You do. I can see it in your eyes when you look at him." Nellie sat on the bed next to Annie and took her by the hand. "He's easy to love. He's kind, and strong, gentle and fierce. All the things you want in a man. If it hadn't been for Blake, I could easily have fallen for Nick."

"He is easy to love." Annie sniffled. "I

wish things were different. I wish we were different. And now, I don't know how he will ever look at me without seeing…oh, Nellie."

"Shh, it'll be fine. Trust me. Now let's get you in the bath and see how you feel after that."

Annie nodded and followed her mutely to the bathroom. Maybe a bath would help. Maybe she could wash his hands off her, wash away the dirty feeling Robert had given her.

She took off the rest of her clothes and left them in a pile on the bathroom floor.

Nellie watched as she got into the tub and then picked up the clothing from the tile.

"Will you be all right here for a bit? I'll get you some clean clothes, lay them on your bed and check back later."

"That's fine." The hot water felt so good as she slid into the tub, almost healing. "I want to soak and scrub myself. Hopefully I'll feel clean again."

Nellie cocked her head. "You get it out of your mind that you are not clean. You are the same woman you were before. Do not let what Robert did to you make you feel anything else. None of this was your fault."

Besides that, I must have known something was wrong. I was going to tell him we needed to include Evie, but I knew he wouldn't want to do that. Then I'd have an excuse not to see him anymore.

"I was eventually going to break it off with him. I just didn't feel like he cared for Evie and I couldn't even contemplate marrying anyone who doesn't love my daughter."

"There you see. It was him not you. Remember that. He did this. Not you."

"I will. Thank you, Nellie. You're a good friend."

"As are you. I'll be back shortly."

Annie watched Nellie leave and lay back in the tub. The hot water felt so good, she closed her eyes. She saw Nick, holding her, soothing her, saving her.

Then the scene changed and Robert was there, forcing himself on her, squeezing her shoulders, ripping her dress, hurting her.

Heart racing, she opened her eyes and sat up in the tub. Grabbing the washcloth and the soap, she scrubbed her body all over. Scrubbed herself hard from head to toe. By the time she was done, she thought she might have scrubbed off all her skin, but at least she felt him gone from her. She felt clean.

Annie got out of the tub and dried off. In her bedroom, Nellie had laid out two outfits, one a lovely green dress that would have matched Nellie's eyes, but looked spectacular with Annie's red hair and pale coloring. The second outfit was her nightgown and robe. How brave was she? Could she face Nick after he'd seen her at her most vulnerable? Having seen her attacked? After him saving her?

Yes, she was not a coward, and as she told Sarah, none of this was her fault. If Annie couldn't face the world now, how would she convince Sarah that she could?

She pulled on her undergarments and then got a black dress from the closet. She pulled her damp hair up into a loose bun at the nape of her neck.

She stopped outside the library, where she knew everyone would be, waiting to see if she made an appearance. Knocking softly on the door, she turned the handle and entered.

The men immediately stood. Nellie stayed where she was on the settee, with her back to Annie.

Nick came to her, folded her hand around the crook in his elbow and placed his hand on top of hers. "Annie, love, are you sure you should be here?" He escorted her to the settee.

"Yes, I need to put that horrendous incident behind me. I'm not letting Robert determine how I feel about myself. If I can't do the things I told Sarah to do, how can I expect her to do them? And she's had it so much worse."

"Sarah?" said Nellie, turning her head toward Annie, with a raised eyebrow.

As she approached, Annie could see that Nellie held Evie.

"Evie, sweetheart, what are you doing awake?"

"I think she knew her mama needed her," said Nellie.

"Oh, yes, I do. I most certainly do." She held her arms out for her daughter.

Evie bounced on Nellie's lap, grinned at her mother and held up her arms to be lifted.

Annie gathered her close. "Oh, Evie, what would I do without you. You are my world. I'd do anything for you."

Nellie brushed the wrinkles from her

skirt. "Who is Sarah?"

"She's my sister," said Nick.

"May I tell them what happened?" asked Annie while she kept her eyes on her bouncing baby girl, who grinned and then babbled, joining the conversation.

"Yes," said Nick, and then perched on the arm of the settee next to Annie.

"Sarah came to The Nugget a couple of nights ago. She'd been beaten badly by her husband and it obviously wasn't the first time. This time though, she left because she's pregnant and wanted to protect her child."

"She'll be staying with me for the foreseeable future," said Nick, clenching his fist. "If that bastard comes around, we'll see how he likes fighting a man."

Annie laid her hand on Nick's leg to calm him then continued with her story. "I told Sarah it would be all right, that none of what happened was her fault. How can I expect her to face what happened to her, if I can't face this? Sarah has suffered for a long time at the hands of her husband, she needs to be safe."

Nick gently squeezed her shoulder. "Annie has been a big help to Sarah. I don't know what I would have done if she hadn't been there."

"You'd have managed, or you'd have come and gotten Nellie. You're a good brother, you'd have figured out a way to help her. What will you do when her husband comes for her? And you know he will. They always do, once they've lost their punching bag. And someone to cook, clean, wash, and in general take care of them."

"How do you know so much about this kind of thing, Annie?" asked Nellie.

She shrugged and swallowed past the lump in her throat. "I saw bruised and battered women in my father's faithful. Often sitting in church right next to their husbands, the very men who gave them the bruises to begin with. They'd sit there and act like nothing was wrong. Like everyone should be sporting black eyes this season. The charade made me sick and there was nothing I could do."

Nellie shook her head. "How awful. Why do they stay?"

"Because they're scared, they have nowhere else to go, but mostly because they've come to believe their attacker. They think they deserve it."

Nellie shook her head, tears glistening in her eyes, "That's horrible."

"We tried to help but sometimes when we did the women were beaten worse. It got to the point where, we were afraid to even talk to some of them for fear their husbands would beat them to death. But that won't happen with Sarah. She has Nick."

Evie started to fuss. She was putting up her hands for Nick to pick her up.

Annie rolled her eyes and smiled. "She always wants to go to you. You must never tell her 'no'."

"Of course, I tell her 'no'. But then she cries and then I soothe her and give her something else."

"Usually his tie." Nellie smiled.

"She does love those things. Has since she was tiny," said Annie, pulling his tie from Evie's mouth. "Do you have any that aren't worn by her chewing on them?"

"Of course. I've learned to keep these ties in the carriage and change into them before I reach here, so she has one of the same few ties to chew on. Sometimes though, she ambushes me. I don't expect her to be somewhere and there you come with her in your arms."

Annie laughed along with everyone else.

Evie hearing the laughter giggled and that made everyone else laugh all the harder.

The evening that started out so awful, turned out to be a good one thanks to her beautiful, funny daughter and Nick. He made Evie laugh, teased her, played with her and entertained them all.

Evie finally got a little fussy and yawned.

"All right, time for you to go to bed little miss," said Annie, taking Evie from Nick.

Evie cried and put her arms out to Nick.

"You go with mama, Sweet Pea." He kissed her nose.

She cried all that much harder when Annie turned to walk away.

"I give up." She turned back toward the group. "Nick would you come with me to put her to bed?"

"Of course. She's used to me putting her to bed when you're not here."

Annie shook her head. The two of them would kill her if she broke them apart and she wouldn't blame them.

They walked in silence to Annie's dressing room which also served as Evie's nursery. Blake had put in a crib and Annie used some of the drawers for Evie's clothes and diapers.

She got out a new set of pajamas and a clean diaper. Annie'd had Blake move a commode into the room, and she padded the top of it and used it to change Evie. It was so much easier than using the crib. Once she had Evie ready for bed, she kissed her, let Nick kiss her and laid her in the crib. Then she wound up the music box that Nick had given her as a baby gift and let it play.

Evie lay quietly with her thumb in her mouth and slowly closed her eyes.

They walked out of the room and Annie left the lamp on in her bedroom with the dressing room door open so if Evie woke she wouldn't be in complete darkness.

"Thank you for helping me put her to sleep. I don't usually have so much trouble."

"It's because I'm here and she's gotten used to me putting her to bed when I'm around. Annie."

"Yes."

"I'm sorry you had to go through what you did tonight. I'm so proud of you handling it like you have. You're a brave, wonderful woman. I thought you should know that." He held her chin up with his knuckle and kissed her tenderly on the lips.

He didn't hold her, didn't make her feel trapped, just gently kissed her.

After all she'd been through, that he would know just what she needed, was wonderful.

It was magical.

CHAPTER 7

Sarah adjusted to living with Nick easily and healed quickly from her ordeal. It had been two weeks and at least the bruises were gone and she smiled more often than not. Annie was teaching her how to cook, while Nick checked with his attorney to see about getting her divorced from John Roland.

Most nights Sarah came to work with Nick. She felt safer being with him and then with Annie in the kitchen. Nick didn't let either of them out into the bar area. He didn't want them to be subjected to possible pawing by some of his clientele.

"Annie, thank you for helping me. I don't know what I'd do without you." Sarah didn't look up from the gravy she was stirring.

"You'd be just fine. And you'll be well and have a healthy baby and a way to make a living on your own if you need to."

"I'll never be as good a cook as you are."

"I'm not good. I just cook simple. You want to taste some sublime cooking, you should come to Blake and Nellie's. Their chef is amazing. They call her Cook but she is so much more than that. She does everything. Bakes bread and sweets, makes succulent, savory stews and soups, and the finest Beef Wellington you've ever tasted."

"Beef Wellington?"

Annie closed her eyes. Her mouth watered as she remembered the last time she'd had Cook's version of the dish. She opened her eyes. "It's a beef tenderloin roast, with liver pate on top, wrapped in a puff pastry and baked. Sometimes it's served with a sauce béarnaise."

"What's that? How will I be able to cook these things if I can't even pronounce them?

"I'll have Nick bring you to dinner and ask Cook to make the dish for you. Then you can talk to her, and she can give you the recipe. She's very generous, willing to share her knowledge."

Sarah finally looked up. "Do you think she'd teach me?"

Annie laughed. "Oh, my cooking isn't good enough now?"

"Who said your cooking isn't good enough?" Nick leaned, arms crossed, against the door frame into the kitchen.

Annie cocked her eyebrow. "How long have you been listening?"

He grinned. "Long enough to hear that I'm bringing Sarah to dinner at Blake and Nellie's."

"Yes," said Annie. "She wants to ask Cook to teach her to be a chef."

Nick nodded. "Good plan, little sister. Learn from the best. Although," he grabbed Annie about the waist and pulled her to him. "Annie is the best as far as I'm concerned." He leaned down and gave her a quick kiss.

Annie's cheeks burned. "Nick. Stop that."

"Nick," said Sally Jo from the doorway. "There's a telegram for Annie."

"Bring it in." He set Annie away from him and met Sally Jo half way. He took the envelope from her and brought it to Annie.

She checked the address on the front,

Annie White, care of Blake Malone, 2809 Greenwich Street, San Francisco, California.

"Sally Jo," Annie called to the woman's retreating back. "Who brought this?"

"James, the Malone's butler dropped it off. I should have told you but I forgot."

"That's all right," said Annie. Then she slipped her finger under the edge and opened the envelope, took out the paper from inside and read.

"Well?" asked Nick. "Is it from your father? What does it say?"

"It says 'No. I'm coming there.' That's all. I'd told him to just say 'no' if he didn't want me to come home. I never expected him to come to California."

"I'm glad he's coming." Nick crossed his arms over his chest. "He can meet me and see for himself that I don't work for the devil."

"Why would he be coming here? I don't understand. Something has got to be wrong."

"Maybe he can't wait to meet Evie," said Sarah.

Nick put his arm around Annie's shoulders but she shrugged him off and walked to the counter opposite him.

"No. That's not like him. He wouldn't spend all that money to come see her. He'd wait until I moved home." She shook her head. "It's something else. Maybe he's dying."

"Now, Annie," Nick walked across the kitchen and wrapped her in his arms. She didn't resist. "You don't know that. Don't get upset by your imagination."

"You're right." She stepped away from Nick and began to pace. "He'll be here in a few weeks. How will I have time to prepare?"

"What are you going to prepare? There's nothing you can do," said Nick, with a shake of his head.

"I know but I feel like I should be doing something."

"Annie, stop." Nick reached out and placed his hands on her shoulders. "You're panicking for no reason. You live a perfectly upstanding life, you take good care of Evie and you are a good friend to everyone you know. What more could your father ask of you?"

"Doesn't your father love you?" Sarah was still stirring the gravy, but removed it from the heat and set the spoon on the plate she had beside the stove for just that purpose.

"Of course, my father loves me." *Why am I so defensive? He does love me. He does.*

"Then why do you fear him so much? You're acting like I did with John. Afraid to make him angry," observed Sarah.

"I'm not afraid." She turned her back to them and stared out the little window next to the kitchen's back door. "I just don't want to disappoint him."

"That's the problem you have with us isn't it? You're afraid you'll disappoint him. It's not because you believe what I do for a living is wrong, but because you're afraid of your father."

"I am not afraid of him!" *Why am I shouting? Is Nick right?*

"Then why are you so upset? You should be happy your father is coming for a visit and instead, you're petrified."

Nick stood there, stiff, his hands clenching and un-clenching.

She knew it was how he controlled his anger.

Annie took a deep breath. "All right, I am worried, I'll give you that but I'm not really afraid. My mother died when I was ten and Father was all I had. He was always wrapped up in his church work, seeing to one member of the church or another. I always came in second. I've always tried my best to make him proud of me."

She didn't realize she was crying until Nick handed her his handkerchief. She looked at him questioningly and he gently wiped his finger across her cheek, showing her the tears there.

"Oh, thank you." She dabbed at her eyes with the cloth.

"Annie." Nick took one of her hands in both of his. "There is no way on earth that your father is not proud of you. He has to be. You're a wonderful woman and I'm sure a perfect daughter."

"You only say that because you want to marry me."

"And now I truly understand your hesitance to accept my proposal. I'll stop pestering you so, until your father gets here. Then I'll have a sit down with him. I'll get his blessing, Annie. I promise I will."

He brought her hand to his lips and placed a soft kiss there.

Shivers ran up and down her spine. *How*

could one little kiss make me feel so much? Make me want more than ever to have Nick for my own? Make me so unhappy?

"What about Evie? Are you going to stop *pestering* her too?" her voice shook.

"I don't pester her, I play with her. Isn't this what you want? You keep saying you can't marry me, well, I'm taking you at your word." He shouted and then softer, more in control, he said, "at least until your father gets here and we get to the bottom of this. My relationship with Evie won't change, just with you. I won't touch you, won't kiss you, and won't keep asking you to marry me. The next time I ask," he warned, his gaze narrowed. "I'll take you at your word and I won't ask again. But I will always be Evie's daddy. Whether you like it or not, she's mine, the daughter of my heart. And she'll always be that."

Eyes filled with tears, Annie nodded her understanding, afraid she'd signed the death warrant on her own happiness.

*****

Annie and Sarah now shared the cooking chores at The Nugget. Sarah was still learning and came to work with Nick every night, so she could learn from Annie.

"Thank you for having Cook make dinner especially for me. The food was wonderful. I don't think I've ever eaten so much or so well."

"She enjoyed showing off her skills. I think if she didn't love the family so much, she'd move on to some place where her talents could be showcased."

"It was so nice—"

The sound of a man shouting came from outside the door to the bar. "Sarah! Sarah! I know you're here. You can't hide from me."

Annie glanced over at Sarah who was white as a sheet.

"Is that your husband?"

Sarah nodded, her arms wrapped around her middle.

"Come with me."

Annie grabbed her by the hand and headed for the back door, which led to the courtyard.

The door from the bar crashed open.

"Sarah! I see you. You can't get away from me."

A large, barrel-chested man with brown hair, came roaring through the doorway. There was no way they could make it outside before he reached them.

Annie grabbed a rolling pin and put herself between Sarah and her husband, John Roland.

"You stay away from her," Annie wielded the rolling pin like a sword. "Just turn around and get out of here."

"You get out of my way, bitch. I'm taking my wife home." He swaggered toward them, his balance a bit off-kilter, he'd obviously been drinking some liquid courage.

Annie raised the rolling pin and brought it down hard but he deflected it with his arm and pushed her back against the stove.

Annie screamed as her hand landed on the hot stove, burning it severely.

He bowled past Annie and grabbed Sarah by the hair.

"You think you can leave me? Sent that lawyer with those divorce papers to sign, did you? You can't leave me. Not ever." He backhanded her, knocking her into the counter.

"Stop that, leave her alone," yelled Annie. She took the cast iron skillet from the stove and bashed him over the head.

The blow didn't stop him. He picked Sarah up by the front of her dress and hit her again.

Sarah slumped to the floor.

He turned to face Annie.

Breathing hard, she held the pan in front of her. "You leave me alone. Leave Sarah alone." She raised the pan and brought it down on his shoulder. He shrugged it off, grabbed the skillet from her and brought it back to hit her with it.

Eyes wide, she watched him, unable to move, knowing he would kill her.

"No!" came a roar from behind John.

Suddenly, he was flying through the air, snatched backwards by his shoulders.

"Nick." Annie breathed a sigh of relief. They were safe now.

John bounced off the wall and slid to the floor. He got up, snarled and barreled toward Nick, shoulders down. He caught Nick in the middle and slammed him against the icebox.

Annie crawled to where Sarah lay in a heap on the floor.

"Sarah. Sarah, sweetie." She smacked Sarah's face lightly. "Wake up."

She came to with a start, whimpered, and curled into a ball.

"It's all right sweetie," said Annie. She

stroked Sarah's uninjured cheek, calming her. "Nick's here, you'll be fine. We're both be fine."

Annie put her arms around Sarah's shoulders. The two of them watched in horror and fascination but mostly with relief as Nick and John fought, sending plates, pans and other kitchen items clattering to the floor.

Then Blake was in the doorway, shouting to John.

"Drop the knife, mister, so I don't have to kill you."

John looked around at Blake, wild-eyed, his gaze flying between Nick and Blake, who held a gun pointed at him.

Suddenly, John plunged at Nick. A shot rang out. John didn't stop. He and Nick grappled for the knife.

Annie saw the blade slice down toward Nick's shoulder.

"No!" she started to shout but then slammed her fist in her mouth so as not to distract Nick.

Nick was on his back on the floor. John straddled him and reared back ready to plunge the weapon deep into Nick's chest, when a second shot, followed in quick succession by a third, rang out.

The knife clattered to the floor and John's lifeless body fell on top of Nick.

"Nick!" Annie shouted and scrambled to her feet. She ran to him.

He'd shoved John's body off and was sitting up.

Annie skidded to a halt and sank to her knees beside him. She looked at him and saw the blood on his clothes.

"You're wounded." She opened his jacket and pulled it off his shoulders and arms. He let her remove it. Then she reached for his tie.

Smiling, Nick grabbed one of her hands. "I'm fine. No major damage."

Annie cocked an eyebrow. "If that's true, why aren't you moving your left arm?"

"Okay, maybe a little damage."

"Let me see. Blake, send for the doctor."

"Blake," said Nick, "don't get the doctor. I'll have one of my staff get him when we get home. He needs to check out Sarah. Are you all right, Sis?"

Annie looked over at Sarah who sat there staring wide-eyed at John's body. "You need to get her out of here. Now. Is your carriage here?"

Nick nodded. "Just out back as always when you're here."

"Then take her home now. She's already seen too much."

"You're coming, too," said Nick, a hand grasped her arm.

Her hand throbbed but that was the least of her worries. "No, I'm fine."

"You're not fine and besides that, Sarah needs you. You're the only friend she has."

Annie nodded. Sarah hadn't been able to make friends when she was married. Her husband never let her. He'd made her life a living hell and made sure she couldn't tell anyone about it.

"Come on, now, let me help you up," Annie reached for his good arm.

Nick shook his head. "You're too small to help me up. I can do it on my own." He put his good hand on the floor and stood.

Annie put his arm over her shoulder and her arm around his waist.

"I don't need your help. As much as I appreciate your concern, but I really have been hurt worse."

She gazed up at him. "Let me see your wound. There's an awful lot of blood. I have bandages, we can help stop the bleeding before the doctor gets out to see you."

He pressed his lips into a tight line. "When we get home."

"No. Now."

She reached up to undo his tie when the feeling in her hand became intense. "Oww." Annie looked down at her left hand. The palm was burnt and small blisters were beginning to pop up. She went to the sink and pumped cold water on her hand.

He followed her and grabbed her hand out of the running water.

"Let me see." His demand allowed no refusal.

"It's all right, just burnt a bit."

"It's blistered. You need to see the doctor. You're definitely coming home with Sarah and me."

"Fine. Lets get going before you bleed to death."

"Would you care?" he asked quietly.

"Don't be stupid." Her eyes filled with tears, whether from the pain of his words or the pain in her hand, she wasn't sure. "Of course, I'd care. Who'd play with Evie?" she quipped, in an effort to keep herself from crying.

He laughed. "You do please me, Annie

mine
."

"I'm sending for the police and get this," Blake nodded toward John Roland's body, "taken care of. You all get out of here. Go home and get the doctor there as soon as possible."

Annie looked over at Nick. He was pale. The loss of blood was becoming apparent.

"We're not going anywhere until we get the bleeding stopped on Nick's shoulder." She took his hand and led him to the chair next to Evie's crib.

"Maybe we *should* do something about it," he finally agreed.

Annie unknotted his tie, unbuttoned his shirt and eased it down and off his arms. The beautiful expanse of his chest was marred by a wound about two inches long, where the knife had sunk deep in his shoulder. Even after this amount of time, the wound was bleeding freely, though not fast. She hurried to the cupboard above the sink and pulled down the bandages she kept there.

When she got back to him, she realized that she didn't have enough cloth to serve as a pad and wrap around his chest, too. He was too large. She took his shirt, folded it and pressed it against the wound.

"Sarah, come help me."

The girl came immediately.

"Press the shirt hard against the wound while I wrap him."

Together they got Nick bandaged and then placed his jacket over his shoulders.

"Now let's go home and get you comfortable to wait for the doctor."

"You said home," said Nick.

"It is home. Your home." She narrowed her gaze. "Don't make more if it than that."

He nodded, disappointment clear on his face.

Annie again put his good arm over her shoulder and her arm around his waist. He leaned on her this time and she welcomed his weight. Nick was weaker than he let on. She could tell by how much he leaned on her.

On the ride home in the carriage, they were all quiet. Annie thought they'd just been through too much and looking at Sarah, she knew she was right.

The woman sat across from her and Nick, staring down at her hands folded in her lap.

Annie touched Sarah's knee. "Honey,

talk to me. What are you thinking?"

She burst into tears and covered her face. "This is all my fault. You're hurt and so is Nick and it's all my fault."

Annie moved to sit next to Sarah and put her arms around her shoulders.

"It's not your fault. John did this, not you."

"But he wouldn't have come if he wasn't looking for me," she practically wailed.

"Maybe, but he would have killed you, and there is no way either Nick or I would let that happen. You are an important part of our lives."

Sarah buried her face in Annie's chest and bawled.

"It's all right. Everything will be all right now." Annie held her close and let her cry.

They arrived at Nick's mansion and his butler opened the carriage door.

"Mr. Cartwright needs your help, sir. He's been wounded," said Annie.

"I'm Philip, madam."

Nick managed to get out of the carriage and then accepted Philip's help into the house.

Sarah and Annie walked in together, holding each other. They followed the butler and Nick to the library where Philip helped the wounded man into one of the large, brown leather chairs in front of the fireplace.

"Send someone for the doctor and get me a blanket for Nick, please, Philip," instructed Annie.

"Yes, madam, right away." He left the room, closing the door behind him.

She went to Nick and put his feet up on the foot stool.

"The doctor will be here shortly and then we'll get you into bed."

"Will you join me?"

"No, I will not. You know better than that."

"But I'm a poor wounded man." He raised his eyebrows and turned down his lips in his best puppy dog look.

"You'll be all right. Now behave, or your sister will get the wrong idea."

Nick laughed but the sound was strained, not his usual rich, booming laugh.

"How are you, Sarah?" asked Annie. "Sit down on the settee. You've been through a lot tonight. Your poor face is bruised again. I can see them starting to form from here."

"I'll be fine Annie. You need to take care of your hand." Sarah looked down at Annie's hand laying open in her lap.

"If I stop using it, it'll dry that way and I won't be able to open it. The pain isn't too bad and blisters have already popped, so it's oozing a bit. I promise to let the doctor look at it when he comes."

"You need to go put it under cold water again. I'll watch Nick until you get back. He is my brother after all."

"Okay, I think it would help. I'll be right back."

Annie left the room, closing the door behind her.

"Nick, are you all right?"

"I'm fine, Sarah. Don't you worry about me. What we need to worry about is you and that baby. You're not having any pain are you?" *Wish I was telling her the truth. Truth is I feel like I'll pass out.*

"Just in my face where John hit me. But nothing I'm not used to."

"That's the thing, little sister. You shouldn't have to be used to that kind of treatment. You won't ever have to face that again. I realize now is not the best time to say this, but John was a wealthy man. You'll inherit everything and men will want to court you because of your money. You'll have to be careful."

"I never knew what kind of money we had. He gave me a household allowance and let me get a new dress once a year at Easter." She smiled and shook her head. "That's probably one of the reasons he was so upset about the baby. He'd have to spend money, buy me a new dress or two as my girth expands."

"Now you can buy a dress whenever you want one. I would suggest you throw out everything you have and buy a whole new, stylish wardrobe. You'll need new things for the baby, too."

Sarah placed her hand protectively over her belly. "I was afraid he would hurt the baby. If you and Annie hadn't intervened, I know I would have lost my little one."

She got off the settee and sat on the floor next to Nick's chair. Then she rested her head on his legs. "Thank you for loving me, brother."

"Always, Sarah. No matter what happens, I'll always love you." Nick rubbed her back with his right hand, soothing her and himself, too.

CHAPTER 8

The doctor came and went. He said Nick's wound was deep but he'd gotten very lucky because no major artery had been cut. He stitched the wound and gave instructions to keep it clean and dry and change the bandages every day.

"Good," Nick announced. "Annie will have to come see me every day now."

"What makes you think I need to be the one to change your bandages?" asked Annie. She sat on the settee, across from him and Sarah. "I happen to be injured, too." She held up her bandaged hand. The doctor had put salve on it and wrapped it loosely.

"No one else knows how," said Nick.

"I'll teach them," countered Annie.

"I'll make sure no one is available to learn," replied Nick.

He was definitely feeling better, or maybe it was the whiskey the doctor administered before stitching him up, or the laudanum he gave him afterward. In any case, Nick was in a playful mood.

"Besides, you have to bring Evie to see me."

"Ah." Annie nodded. "Now we get now to the real reason. My beautiful daughter."

Nick grinned. "I admit it. I can't go without seeing my baby girl."

Annie smiled. The way he said it, the wistfulness in his voice, touched Annie so deeply, it brought tears to her eyes. And the question arose again, how could she part them? Doing so would be beyond cruel.

"All right, I give up. Evie and I will come and change your bandages every day before I go to work."

Nick shook his head. "No. You won't be working until your hand is healed and I can go with you. There's no getting around it. I'll ask Blake to tell Flossie she'll be doing the cooking. She's been learning from you and is anxious to try her hand at cooking the meals anyway. So let her and let your hand heal."

Her shoulders slumped. Defeated again. And yet, she perked back up, it would give her an opportunity to spend some quiet time with Nick and Sarah. Learn more about their childhoods.

"Fine. Evie and I will come over every day to check your wound and check in on Sarah."

Annie looked pointedly at Sarah who sat on the floor next to Nick. "How are you, Sarah? The doctor said you and the baby are fit, physically, just bruised, but how do you *feel*?"

"I'm actually doing well." Sarah, rubbed Nick's leg absentmindedly. "John can't hurt me or my baby any longer. I know I should be feeling something for him, but all I feel is relief. Is that wrong?"

"No, not at all. You've been through a lot," said Annie. "When I lost my husband, even though I didn't love him, I was relieved and I felt guilty because I didn't feel more remorse. But all I could bring myself to feel was liberated. And when I found out what he'd done to us financially, I was so angry I couldn't see straight. But then I had Evie, and my feelings toward

William softened. I was still thankful that he was dead, but he'd given me my greatest love as well. I was grateful for her even more than I was angry at him."

"When my baby is born," said Sarah. "I know I will feel the same way. Maybe I already do. It's the only good thing to come of my marriage. This baby, she'll know her mama loves her. No matter what, she'll always be my baby."

"And I'll have two little ones to spoil," said Nick, weakly.

The tremor in his voice alarmed Annie. She stood and went to him. Bending slightly, she placed her hand on his forehead.

"You're burning up, Nick. We need to get you to bed. Now. Sarah, ring the bell for Philip. We'll need his help."

The butler entered the library minutes later.

"You rang, madam."

"Yes, we need to get Nick to his bedroom and into bed. I need your help to do so."

"Of course." He approached Nick, who'd managed to stand and was now leaning on Annie. "Come Mr. Cartwright.

Lean on me and we'll get you upstairs."

They got Nick to his bedroom, then Annie stopped and turned to Sarah.

"Please get some washcloths, towels and a basin of ice chips. There should already a pitcher of water in the room or we can get it from the bathroom."

"Right away," said Sarah.

Annie pulled the covers down on the bed and fluffed the pillows.

Philip had Nick down to his underdrawers and turned to Annie. "You might want to turn around, madam, while I get him into bed."

She turned around but said, "No need to worry about my sensibilities, Philip, I've been a married woman, there's nothing Nick has that I haven't seen before."

"You wound me, madam," said Nick. Then he chuckled. "I think I may surprise you."

Annie couldn't help but look after a statement like that and when she did her jaw dropped. Nick was magnificently built, in all ways. She knew he had broad shoulders, a slender waist and long, muscled legs. She saw all of that with his clothes on, but his man parts...well...goodness. William was not that endowed.

"Surprise," said Nick, softly.

"You are just a man. Nothing more." Annie said with bravado, after regaining her wits.

"Again, you wound me, madam."

"Impossible. Now lie down and let me get started cooling you down."

"That, m'dear is not possible, when you are around. However, I do feel extremely tired suddenly and think lying down would be the best thing."

Philip helped him into the bed and Annie pulled the sheet over him, for modesty's sake, though she wondered why she bothered.

As soon as Nick's head hit the pillow he was asleep. Passed out was more like it.

Sarah returned with the basin of ice and the linens.

"What do you want me to do? I need to help."

Annie pulled the sheet from the foot of the bed and brought it up, so that only Nick's private parts were covered.

"You can start rubbing down his legs with the cold water. I'll do his chest and arms. We need to get the fever to break."

Sarah didn't say a word, not about Nick's nakedness or anything else, she just poured water from the pitcher into the basin of ice and then soaked two washcloths in the icy water, wrung them out and handed one to Annie. She appeared to be determined to help her brother in any way possible.

Both women worked into the night. Finally Annie, seeing Sarah's exhaustion, said, "Sarah, honey, go to bed. You've got to think of the babe. You need your rest and I had Philip send someone to Blake and Nellie to tell them I'm staying here. I'll continue with Nick. Don't worry. I think he's getting better."

She lied. The fever still raged through him, but Sarah needed rest and Annie knew if she thought her brother still needed her, she would wear herself ragged.

"If you're sure, I would like to lie down for awhile."

"Of course. I'll come wake you when I need a break. Fair enough?"

Sarah smiled. "Fair enough."

Annie took a deep breath. The night would be a long one.

*****

Nellie came by the next morning with

Evie. "I'm sorry. I'm running out of milk. I'm not used to nursing two infants."

Annie met Nellie in the foyer and took Evie from her. Her breasts hurt from not nursing and she hoped Evie was hungry. "Don't be sorry. I'm the one who should apologize for taking advantage of you. It's probably time I weaned her anyway. I've had to supplement with regular food, eggs, oatmeal, mashed potatoes and the like, for a while now. She doesn't get full on milk alone."

Nellie nodded. "I know what you mean. Daniel is the same way. How's Nick? Blake told me what happened and you look exhausted."

"I'm fine but he's not good. His fever is still high. Sarah and I have been rubbing him down with ice water but it doesn't seem to help much. I've given him laudanum for the pain and the medicine does allow him to sleep. But I worry about the fever. His wound is infected and even though I clean it every day, I don't think I'm getting out the infection. But it's all I can do."

"Did you send for the doctor again?"

Annie nodded. "Yes. He said we're basically doing everything that can be done.

He sprayed carbolic acid on the wound and said that would help with the infection."

"Do you have any willow bark tea? That helps with fever and pain."

Evie grew restless and Annie bounced her on her hip.

"I'll ask Philip about the tea. Thank you for bringing Evie to me. Maybe she'll make him feel better. If nothing else, she'll help Sarah forget the awfulness of last night. She feels it's her fault."

"But it's not. Do you want me to talk to her? I could tell her my story. She needs to know that nothing she's ever done could account for what she's been through."

"I'm sure it would, but right now she needs to be involved in getting Nick better. It will help her to realize she didn't do this, her husband did. I really need to get back to Nick."

"Of course. Have Philip send word if you need anything from us."

Nellie and Annie hugged with Evie between them. She fussed a little but was soon all smiles again.

Annie mounted the stairs to Nick's bedroom with Evie in her arms.

"I thought maybe you'd gone," he said

when she entered.

"Not yet. How are you feeling? Up to seeing your favorite girl?"

"My favorite girl has always been beside me. I know you and Sarah have been trying to keep me cool."

"Well, Sarah needed to rest. She has to take care of herself and the baby."

"What about you, Annie? Don't you need to rest, too?"

She gazed into his brown eyes, bright with fever. "You needed me more."

She placed Evie on the bed and the baby immediately crawled up to Nick. Evie kissed Nick and lay down next to him with her head on his uninjured shoulder.

Nick wrapped his arm around her and held her close.

"Do you suppose she knows you're hurt?" wondered Annie. "Or maybe she's just missed you."

"It's only been a day. She couldn't miss me."

Annie cocked her head and smiled as she stood by the bed and watched the two most important people in her life, cuddle. "I don't know, she's used to seeing you every day. A whole day is a long time in her life."

"I suppose. I'm just glad you're both here."

"Where else would I be? I can't let Sarah try to take care of you alone. She has enough to deal with. She blames herself for all this. I keep telling her it's not her fault but I don't think she believes me."

Nick sighed deeply.

Annie was sorry she'd mentioned Sarah at all.

"Don't worry about her. I'll make sure Sarah is okay. You just concentrate on getting well yourself."

Nick smiled and shook his head. "When I dreamed of us spending our first night together in my bedroom, this is not what I had in mind.

He was outrageous. To be honest this wasn't how she'd pictured their first night together either. Even though she knew there couldn't be a first night for them, she had her dreams.

*****

For three days Nick's fever spiked and eased. He would get cooler and become more lucid, and then the next thing Annie knew he was hallucinating, trying to get out of bed and open the windows.

She was afraid to leave him alone. He wouldn't calm for anyone but her when he was in the grips of his fever. He wouldn't listen to Sarah at all. The poor girl had awakened Annie on two different occasions when Nick, naked as a jay bird, was calling for her and threatening to search the house until he found her. Annie was afraid Sarah might be scarred for life seeing him like that.

On the third night, Evie woke when Sarah came in. Nick was at it again. When Annie finally dressed and she and Evie got to Nick's room she found him sitting in front of the cold fireplace, naked and shivering. The fever had apparently broken and left him chilled.

"Nick! Get into bed this minute. You'll catch your death. We just got you over one fever, you don't need another."

She set Evie on the floor, on the blanket she kept there just for her and then went to Nick.

"So co...cold," he said through chattering teeth.

"I know you're cold. Come with me."

Annie held out her hand and tried to ignore his naked state. She'd been trying to ignore it for three days and doing so was difficult. Nick was a magnificent specimen of a man. William had been handsome, there was no denying that, but Nick put him to shame.

She closed her eyes and gritted her teeth before pulling him out of the chair and leading him to bed.

"Annie, lay with me. Help me."

"I can't lay with you."

"You can keep on your clothes, I just need your closeness."

"We'll see. Get into bed and let me try to get you warm."

He lay in the bed and she covered him folding the blankets and bedspread in half and so doubling the amount of blankets over him. Then she and the baby lay down next to him, on top of the sheet. She rolled to his side and cuddled with him. Evie lay between them, and the three of them slept, at ease for the first time in days.

*****

"Annie. Annie wake up," whispered Sarah.

"What is it Sarah? Nick is fine, see?" She patted the mound of covers, covers that she was suddenly aware she was under.

"Annie there's a man and woman downstairs to see you. He says he's—"

"Your father."

The deep, resonate voice, familiar from so many sermons, caused Annie to bolt upright in the bed and look toward the doorway. She thought she must be having a nightmare but the vision seemed awfully real. Evie took that moment to sit up and kick all the blankets off. It was easy to see that Nick was nude underneath all the covers.

"Oh, God," Heat invaded her cheeks, and Annie buried her face in her hands.

"Do not take the Lord's name in vain, Daughter. Get out of that sinful bed and meet me downstairs. This young woman will direct me to your," he nodded towards Nick, "friend's library."

"Yes, sir," said Sarah with a curtsey. "Follow me."

Her father turned toward the door and then with a glance back, shook his head and took a deep breath.

Annie rolled off the other side of the bed, stood and then grabbed Evie.

"What's the hurry now, Annie? He's already seen what he saw and I'm sure has made up his mind. There's not anything you can do to change it," said Nick, his voice laden with sleep.

"This is not the way I wanted my father to meet you," she hissed. "I've got to take care of Evie, she's soaked and you probably are too. Please do your best to clean up and wait for me to go with you to the library."

"We'll see."

The calculated look on his face didn't make Annie feel any better.

She rolled her eyes and let out a deep sigh. This was not going well. "Just get up."

She turned and left the room with Evie. When she got to her room, she cleaned the baby up and changed her wet diaper, put her in her cutest outfit, and readied her to meet her grandfather.

After Evie was ready, Annie put her in her crib, the one Nick kept 'just in case' he had Evie, so she wouldn't get dirty. Then Annie washed her face, brushed her hair, and put on her cleanest dress, a light blue gingham. She didn't have many to choose from. Nellie had only brought three, thinking, as Annie did, that she'd be home soon. She examined herself in the mirror over the vanity. Her stomach was tied in knots and she was pale, more so than usual. Meeting her father like this did nothing good for her complexion. Annie pinched her cheeks and bit her lips.

"That's better," she said to her reflection.

Getting Evie, she left the room and walked down the stairs to the library. She didn't bother to stop by Nick's room. She knew he'd already gone downstairs. He wasn't about to leave her father alone. Today her destiny would be determined, whether she liked it or not.

CHAPTER 9

Annie stopped outside the library and took a deep breath, then turned the knob.

"You kept us waiting, Daughter. And why are you not still in mourning?"

Her tall, slender father stood at one end of the fireplace, a short, plump woman next to him. Nick leaned against the sidebar across the room from her father. His arms were crossed and Annie knew that had to hurt. He managed to dress in his pants, shoes and a shirt that was open at the neck. She knew a tie was beyond him right now.

"I have my reasons for not wearing black, Father."

He ignored her response.

"Daughter," her father boomed in that

voice of his. "Before we begin to speak of your behavior, I want you to meet someone. This is Doris. Doris Markum, your new stepmother."

"Stepmother?" *After all these years?*

"Yes, Annabelle Leona," said her father using her full name.

He never did that unless he was angry at her. *Was it her fault he'd never married before?*

"Your stepmother. We're on our honeymoon trip and thought we'd stop in San Francisco and surprise *you*, not the other way around."

Evie was starting to fuss. She wanted down so she could go to Nick. Annie ignored her.

"Mama" said Evie and kicked her legs. She leaned over Annie's arm.

"Evie? Did you just say Mama? Yes, you did. You are a good girl," exclaimed Annie. She turned to Nick. "Did you hear? She said 'Mama'."

He grinned. "I heard. She's a smart girl."

"Daughter, your attention, please," said her father, obviously not impressed with Evie's first words.

"Yes, Father. You're on your

honeymoon trip?" Annie, stared at the heavily made-up woman next to her father. "How could you afford a trip of any kind much less for a honeymoon?"

"That would be my doing, dear," said Doris. Her nasally voice grated on Annie's already frayed nerves. "I came into some money when I sold my circus, and Hyrum and I are using some of that to sail around the world."

Annie finally put down Evie so she wouldn't drop her.

"Circus!? You owned a circus?"

"Now, Annie," began her father with a hand held upright. "Don't make judgments."

Annie was furious. A circus was not any different in her father's eyes than a saloon or at least, that's what he'd taught her all these years.

Evie immediately crawled to Nick. "Dada" she said as she pulled herself up on his pant leg.

"Hello, Sweet Pea." He bent down and picked her up with his right arm. His left arm in a sling.

Annie noticed the grimace he made when he picked up Evie and almost went to him.

"You've taught me…" Annie took a breath. "All these years you've taught me that only evil resided in saloons and circuses and the like. Now you've married the owner of one. And you tell me not to make judgments when that's exactly what you've done based on what you thought you saw. You didn't ask me what happened or what I was doing. You made a snap judgment."

"Stop this right now, Daughter," her father roared.

Nick stepped up to Annie's side with Evie.

"You will not talk like that to Annie. She deserves your admiration and respect and you'll treat her with such."

Annie turned her face up to Nick, thank you on her lips, but she didn't get the chance to say it. Nick was ashen. Immediately, Annie took Evie from him and handed her to her grandfather.

"Nick, you should still be in bed." She put her arm around his waist and guided him to the chair by the fire. "I'm so sorry I made you come down here."

"Don't worry about it. You know I won't let you face him alone."

Tears formed in her eyes, but she

refused to let them fall. She helped him to sit and then noticed blood seeping through his shirt. "Your wound is open. It's bleeding. Let's get your shirt off."

"Annie, your father," whispered Nick.

She thought for a fleeting moment what was more important, her father or Nick. The answer was easy. Nick. "Father, you will say nothing. You will go and pull the bell cord to summon Philip. Then you will hold your granddaughter and keep her occupied."

"Did I hear right? Did this child call him 'Dada'?"

"I believe she did. Today is the first time she's said anything other nonsense babbling."

"He is the child's father?"

"I am not discussing this with you right now. I'm checking on Nick's wound and when I've gotten him back to bed, then I might deign to talk to you."

Her father handed the baby to Doris.

Evie looked at Doris and smiled. Then she started playing with her necklace.

"Let me help you get him back upstairs to his bed," said her father.

"Not until I've seen the wound. I need to know—"

"You can do that when the man is back in bed. I'll help you. Come young man," said Hyrum.

Philip entered the library.

"You rang, madam?"

"Yes. Bring bandages and willow bark tea to Mr. Cartwright's room. Have Sarah meet us there."

"All right, Father, let's go."

"Give me your arm, young man and let's get you out of that chair and back into bed. I can see there is more to this story than I first saw."

"Yes, sir," said Nick. "A lot more."

Hyrum and Nick mounted the stairs, with Annie leading the way. When she reached Nick's room, she pulled back the covers on the bed.

"Let's get you out of those clothes and into the bed." She bent to remove his shoes.

"Daughter, I'll get him undressed and you will turn your back and act with a modicum of decorum."

Annie rolled her eyes, but did as her father asked. She wasn't about to tell him she knew exactly what Nick looked like naked. That was more information than he needed right now.

"You can turn around now."

Annie went to the bed and put her inside wrist on Nick's forehead.

"You're still cool, so the fever hasn't returned, but you've opened your wound. I'll clean it and rewrap it. Then I want Philip to call the doctor and have him look at it."

"Don't leave me, Annie. Please." Nick put his hand on her arm, and his brown eyes beseeched her.

"I won't leave until you're well enough to do for yourself. Then we'll talk. Let's get off these bandages."

She had everything she needed either on top of the bureau or on his nightstand, bandages, pads, and scissors. She used the scissors to cut through the cloth and remove it. The wound was angry red and she wasn't sure it was still infected. The doctor would have to tell her.

Sarah came into the room carrying the tea and the wrappings.

"Where is Philip?" asked Annie.

"He's getting the doctor. I told him I could do this."

Annie nodded. Sarah was becoming more confident and that was good. Only a week had passed since the attack, but her bruises were healing and so was her spirit.

"Father. This is Sarah. Nick's sister. You *will* be kind to her. Nick Cartwright is the man in the bed whose home you barged into."

"Of course, I will. What must you think of me? Pleased to meet you, young woman," said Hyrum with a nod of his head.

"Hmpft" huffed Annie and went back to caring for Nick.

"And you, sir," said Sarah back, though she looked as afraid of Hyrum Markum as she had been her husband.

Annie didn't blame her. She was afraid of her father, though she wouldn't admit that to anyone and sometimes not even to herself. As for Sarah, maybe she'd be extra cautious for a while with all men she didn't know, but Annie didn't think that was a bad thing.

"What can I do to help, Daughter?"

"Go entertain and get to know your granddaughter." Annie turned to her father. "She's a bright, funny baby. You'll love her if you give her a chance."

Her father frowned and cocked his head. "Of course, I love her. She's your daughter. How could I do anything else?"

Annie smiled and nodded. "How indeed?" She watched his retreating form as he went through the door, then turned back to Nick.

"It was too soon for you to be out of bed. I should have insisted that you stay where you were. I'm so sorry, Nick."

Nick took her hand in his. "Don't be. I wouldn't let you face your father alone."

Annie grinned, eased that the color had returned to Nick's face. "Did you hear Evie?"

Nick's face formed a wide smile. "Dada. She knows."

"You're all she's ever had for a father. Of course, she'd call you Dada."

"Not true. There's Blake but she didn't call him that, she said it to me. She knows, Annie. I'm her father. Maybe not by blood, but by every other means necessary."

"I'm not arguing with you. You have been. She loves you, I daresay almost as much as you love her."

She pulled the bandage away from the injury. Some of the dried blood and pus stuck to it but Nick didn't flinch. Annie dipped her washrag into the basin of hot water Sarah put by the bed. She got the washcloth soapy with the lye soap she'd put next to the basin. "I'm going to clean this up and it may hurt some, but I'll be as gentle as I can."

She cleaned and rinsed, cleaned and rinsed, until the wound seeped only blood.

"That looks much better."

"The doctor is here," said Sarah entering the room with the doctor behind her.

"Doctor Walsh," Annie pulled a dry towel out of the linen pile and dryed her hands. "I'm so glad you could come back. I think his shoulder got infected."

"Let me see, Annie." The doctor examined the wound, poking and prodding with his fingers, squeezing a little here and there. "I think you've got it good and clean. I'm going to spray some carbolic acid on it and hope that will take care of the rest of the infection. Now I'll let you bandage him up and then I expect him to sleep. And by the looks of it, you too."

"I'm fine, Doctor. Actually I got several hours rest last night. First time in a few days."

"We both did," said Nick.

"Well, Nick, I want you to take some laudanum. I've got it here." He put several drops in the glass of water on the nightstand. "Here now, drink it down."

Nick obeyed and drank all of the liquid.

"I see you have what looks like willow bark tea here. You should drink that, Annie. It will help you sleep and help the pain in your hand. I know it must hurt."

"I haven't really noticed and I don't take laudanum or willow bark tea. I have a baby to take care of, and I have to be there for her."

The doctor nodded. "Well, you do the best you can. Try to sleep when he does and don't let him wear you out. I don't think he'll be getting anymore fevers, so you should take care of yourself for a while."

"Thank you. I do appreciate you coming out on such short notice," said Annie.

"Yeah, Doc, thanks," said Nick. His eyes were already getting heavy and is words a little slower than usual.

"Try to keep him calm. If that wound continues to seep let me know. It should get better soon now. I've left you liniment to put on it after you change the bandage next time. It will help the wound heal, and keep the pads you cover the injury with from sticking and starting the process all over again."

"Thank you so much."

Doctor Walsh pulled her aside. "I hope Nick knows how much you're sacrificing for him. There is already talk around town. The fact that you cook at The Nugget doesn't distract from the fact that you are also William White's widow and people do talk. You've been here for a week, unchaperoned."

She raised her eyebrow and let out a sigh. "I'm not unchaperoned. Nick's sister Sarah is here. Besides, I don't care what those people think of me and I don't care about being William's widow. He left me debts and the title to a ship that is supposed to have sunk. He left me nothing. And those people you're talking about did nothing to help. If it weren't for Nellie and Blake and yes, Nick, I'd be living on the streets with Evie."

The doctor shook his head. "I'm sorry my dear, I shouldn't have brought it up."

"No, it's all right but when you talk to those fine upstanding people who are whispering about me behind their hands, tell them I'm good, no thanks to them. I thought they were William's friends, but that proved not to be true. When it came out that our fortune had been lost they stopped coming to visit. They were nowhere to be found when William died. Those people knew things I didn't not. I was blindsided by our dire financial situation. "

"I will. Now that I've got you fired up, you can go talk to your father."

Her head popped up and she glanced toward the door. "What? How did you know?"

"I caught a bit of the exchange before I came in and Philip told me that he was here…unexpectedly."

"Yes, that's putting it mildly. I still don't know how he found me. But if I don't talk to him I won't find out will I?" She waved her hand toward the door. "Come, I'll walk you down."

After she showed the doctor out, Annie went to the library. She opened the door to her father's booming laugh followed by Evie's squeal of delight.

"Well, it looks like you two are getting on."

Evie walked around the coffee table. She did it without falling and looked so proud of herself when her grandfather clapped and praised her. She grinned and bounced up and down as fast as her chubby legs would let her.

"She's marvelous. Absolutely smart as a whip, just as you were at her age."

Annie grinned. "I'm glad to hear you remember when I was her age. I think she's absolutely the smartest, most beautiful baby there is, and Nick thinks the same thing. He's absolutely smitten with her." She didn't look at her father for his response, but said quietly, "He saved my life, how could I do any less for him?"

"Ah, but you love him do you not, Daughter?"

"Yes, very much."

"Why haven't you married him?"

She paused and took a deep breath. "Because he owns and runs a saloon. One that I work at as a cook, but I've been taught all these years that only the work of the devil is done in saloons...and circuses." Eyebrow raised, she looked pointedly at Doris. "What's changed, Father? And how did you find me?"

"A kind woman named Nellie Malone gave us this address when we stopped at her home. That was the last address we had for you."

"Ah, of course. I sent my letter with that address for your response. I didn't know where I would be but knew that Blake, Nick's partner and my best friend's husband would find me."

She looked around and saw that no one was sitting. "Come sit, be comfortable. I'll ring for Philip to bring us tea." She walked over to the bell cord and pulled gently.

Philip opened the door momentarily. "Yes, madam."

"Can you please get us some coffee, tea and several of the pastries Cook made for us yesterday."

"Yes, madam. Right away."

Annie sat in one of the leather chairs and left the settee for her father and Doris.

"So tell me how you met."

"My circus came to town and some of my people, including me, attended your father's church while we were there. The courtship happened very quickly. I admit I fell for him the first time I heard that wonderful voice of his. I've a terrible voice."

Annie opened her mouth to protest, then closed it again.

"Don't worry about offending me, I

know what I sound like."

"Hyrum, didn't let that stop him. He was determined to save me. And I was determined to be saved, as long as it was by him." She reached over and patted his knee.

Her father blushed.

Annie had to look twice, she'd never seen him blush before. It made her smile.

"After we married, I decided I didn't want to run the circus anymore. I sold it to my ringmaster and performers. They bought it together, so it wouldn't have to close." She looked at Hyrum. "You see I was determined, one way or another, to spend my life with your father."

Annie raised her eyebrows. "And you, Father, did you give up your congregation?"

"In a manner of speaking. I'm taking a sabbatical. Many of the places we will be visiting are holy sites and I plan on studying while I'm there."

"I wish you both the best."

"What about you, Daughter? Tell me what is happening in your life. I was very surprised to find out you had been widowed and had a child. It was only a short while ago that you wrote but it would appear that things have changed, somewhat."

Annie told them about William leaving her broke, about Nellie taking her in, about being courted by Nick and working at The Nugget to get money to go back to New York.

By the time she finished, she was crying.

Hyrum rose walked to his daughter, and took her in his arms.

"I'm sorry you've had such a bad time of it. I wish I could have been here for you."

"Nick has been here for me."

"Ah yes, Nick. I guess we'd better get to that now, shouldn't we? You know it is totally improper the situation that I found you in." He set her away from him and crossed his arms over his chest. "You and Evie in bed with a naked man, does not a happy father make."

"I wasn't in bed with him. Well, I was, but not the way you think. I was simply easing him. I was fully clothed for Pete's sake." She shook her head and clenched her teeth, making her jaw ache. "He's been in so much pain, battling fever and chills. I wanted to give him some comfort. And yes, I admit, I relished it. I slept, really slept for the first time in days. He did as well. And Evie was between us. For goodness sake, we were extremely well-chaperoned with her there."

"I question that." Her father, cocked an eyebrow. "She seems to be quite enamored with the man."

Annie smiled. She couldn't help it. Whenever she thought of Nick and Evie, she smiled. "He is of her as well. He loves her as much or more than any father could. He's been there for her since the night she was born."

Hyrum frowned. "What was he doing at my granddaughter's birth?"

"He happened to be there when I got to Nellie and Blake's home. It wasn't too long after I arrived that I began to have labor pains and shortly after that Evie was born."

"But he was in love with you before that. Or am I mistaken."

Annie closed her eyes and nodded her head. "You're not mistaken. He says he's loved me since the first time he met me at Nellie and Blake's wedding. I married William soon after. There was never any love between William and I, but I thought there was mutual respect and trust. I was fully prepared to live my life with only that. Without love." She furrowed her brows.

"But I was wrong. Father, he left me with nothing but debt and the title to a sunken ship. I had to sell almost everything in order to pay his bills."

"What do you intend to do now?"

"I don't know. Everything I believed has been turned on end. I don't know what to think, what to believe. I can't just throw away twenty-four years of learning."

"You don't need to throw it away. That which you learned has not changed. Doris sold her circus, for me, for my beliefs."

Doris shook her head. Her blue flowered hat was tied under her chin but still bounced with the movement of her head.

"I only sold it partially for you, Hyrum," said Doris. "I was ready to get out of the business. It just happened to be a good time when I fell in love with you."

"So are you saying you still believe that a saloon is a den of the devil? And that those who work there are doing his work, even though you married a woman who owned a circus?" asked Annie.

"Of course, I do. I've not amended my views," her father confirmed.

"Why can't you understand? The people at a saloon are just people. Trying to get by, trying to make a living. Do you think I'm doing the devil's work because I work there as a cook?"

Her father paused. "I have not changed my mind and nothing that I've seen here has given me evidence to change. Nothing I saw at The Nugget, has given me evidence to change. If anything, seeing the scantily-clad women and the men getting falling down drunk only reaffirms my beliefs."

Annie stood, walked to the wall and pulled the bell cord. "I think you should leave. I can see we have nothing to discuss, if you will not admit there could be good people working in the places you call parts of Hell. "

"But, we just got here, Daughter."

"My name…is *Annie,*" she said it through clenched teeth, but she wanted to shout, to scream at him and maybe get his attention. "You don't know me. You've never known me because you've never wanted to. I hope you're both very happy in the fantasy world you've made for yourself."

"Annie, please," said her father opening his arms like he was giving a sermon. "I'm not unbending. Show me why I should. Help me to see what you see."

Tears dropped onto her dress front. The thought of losing her father forever was almost more than she could bear. She nodded and sniffled. "When Nick is well, you can come talk to him and Blake, his partner. See the kind of businesses they have. They have one called an amusement park that is for families. They are not wicked people. You will see that, if you let yourself."

"I'll try to remain open, for your sake."

She wiped her eyes with the hanky she kept up her sleeve. "Where are you staying?"

"At the Plaza Hotel. We have reservations for the next three weeks. Our intention was to visit with you and do some sightseeing while we're here. Perhaps go to the gold fields and preach a sermon or two."

"There is a shanty town where my friend Nellie helps out. She and some of the other wealthy ladies in the city are fund-raising to build an orphanage. I'm sure Reverend Schossow would be amenable to having you guest-speak at his church. He's a kind man."

Philip entered the room. "You rang, madam?"

"Yes, my mistake, Philip. Forgive me. I'll show my father out myself."

"As you wish." Philip bowed his head, turned and left the room, closing the door behind him.

"I do have to go and attend to Nick." I won't let him change my mind. Regardless of what you think, I'm not leaving him as long as he needs me here. He saved my life. I owe him so much more than I can ever repay."

"I can see you believe that, and I do think you're a woman of your word and of honor." He frowned. "I'll not question you, though, I still don't like it."

"Thank you, Father." Annie stood on tiptoe and kissed her father's cheek. "I'll contact you when he's better.

CHAPTER 10

"He's agreed to get to know you before he passes judgment," said Annie, cheerfully. She sat next to the bed in a rocking chair she'd had Philip bring from the parlor downstairs.

"How gracious of him," Sarcasm fairly dripped from Nick's words. He sat, propped up in the bed with pillows. It had been almost a week now since his fever broke and having to stay in bed made him restless.

"Considering his beliefs, it *is* gracious of him. He could have refused to see or talk to you."

"Why didn't he? What did you tell him to make him give me a chance? Hmm?" He smiled wide. "Could it have been that you love me? You do you know. I know you do."

"I don't," Annie knew her lie wasn't very believable because she always blushed something awful when she told a lie, even a little one. And this wasn't a little one, it was a spectacular untruth.

"You're blushing, Annie mine. Why are you blushing if you're so sure you don't love me?"

"You always make me blush. The things you say are simply outrageous, that's all."

He chuckled. "Deny it all you wish, but I know the truth."

Annie stood. "I'm not arguing with you. I'm checking on Evie. She'll be upset if she's awake too long and by herself. She'll be hungry, too."

"Bring her in here. I don't mind watching you nurse."

She rolled her eyes. "Of course, you don't. I'll feed her before I come back and I'll order lunch for you to be brought up. What do you want?"

"Well, what do you think Evie will want to share with me?"

"As long as it's from you, she'll eat anything."

"Then I want a chicken sandwich, with

mashed potatoes and cookies for dessert."

"All her favorites. You spoil her."

"That's what I'm here for."

Annie shook her head and left. As she walked back to her room and her daughter, she couldn't help but imagine what her life would be like if she lived here and was married to Nick. She would love that so much, but she still wasn't willing to go against all that she knew, all beliefs she'd grown up with. And her father...it didn't seem to matter that Doris used to own a circus, she'd sold it and therefore had redeemed herself in her father's eyes.

She couldn't ask Nick to sell The Nugget. It was his livelihood. There was nothing else for him. Blake managed the amusement park and family emporium. There wasn't a need for two managers as it wasn't open twenty-four hours a day like the saloon was.

Their love just wasn't meant to be. She had to resign herself to that fact. Resign herself to living alone. Just her and Evie, for the rest of her days. There was no way she could marry anyone else, loving Nick as she did.

*****

Nick was out of bed and Annie's hand was much better. It had been ten days and all the blisters had broken and healed. There would be terrible scarring. She'd never have lovely hands again, but that didn't matter.

"Let me see your hands," commanded Nick at the breakfast table. Tonight was to be their first night back at work.

"You've already seen them. They haven't changed. They are healed enough for me to go back to work. If Sarah is there to help me, things will be fine. If she isn't ready then I'll have Flossy help me."

"If Sarah isn't ready for what?" asked the woman in question as she entered the room and made her way to her chair at Nick's left side. Her bruises were healed and she seemed happier than Annie had ever seen her before.

"Ready to go back to work," said Annie who sat on Nick's right. He said it was appropriate as that's where a man's partner should be. She scooped a forkful of scrambled eggs into her mouth and chewed. After swallowing, she asked, "Have you stolen Cook from Blake and Nellie? The food has been wonderful."

Nick laughed. "Blame Philip. He had a

cousin come into town from Ireland who needed a job. The woman is a cook and so, we now have a real cook. Her name is Bridget."

"Well, Philip," Annie said to the butler standing sentinel against the wall. "You tell Bridget that this is a wonderful meal. I look forward to all her efforts."

"Yes madam. I will."

"Does that mean you're staying?"

"I'm staying one more night. I'll pack up and go back to Nellie's tomorrow."

Nick frowned, almost pouting. "Why wait?"

Her jaw clenched as anger suddenly radiated through her. "I had thought to give Evie another day with you, but if you'd rather, I'll go pack our bags now and your driver can take us home." She slapped her napkin down on the table and stood.

Nick grabbed her arm. "No. Wait. I'm sorry. Of course, I want you to stay. For as long as you like."

She relaxed, sat back down and replaced her napkin in her lap. "Thank you. I want to give Evie as much time as she can have with you." She shook her head. "Evie's connection to you is good for her. It's been there since the day she was born and you took her from Blake. First time you'd ever held a baby, and yet she stopped crying when you took her. It was as though she was being held by her daddy and she knew it. She loves you and needs you so much."

He reached over and took her hand in his.

She tried to bring it back.

"Don't. Don't hide your hands from me. They carry marks of your bravery. If not for you…"

"I'd be dead," said Sarah as she rose to return to the sideboard for more food.

"Your appetite seems to have returned," teased Annie.

The girl reddened. "I find that I'm very hungry lately."

"That won't change for some time. Even after the baby's born, you'll eat more than you used to because you're making milk for her."

"You both keep referring to the baby as a her," said Nick. "How can you know? And what if it's a boy? Will you love it less?"

"No, of course I won't." Sarah lifted her chin. "If it's a boy I'll love him and teach him to be a real man. To treat women with respect and never to hit one."

"Basically to be the opposite of his father," said Annie. Her anger at Sarah's husband, John, for all the injury he caused had not subsided just because the man was dead.

"Exactly." Sarah smiled. "I won't have any son of my growing up thinking that kind of behavior is acceptable."

Nick took Sarah's hand and squeezed it. "You've grown so much, Sis. I'm proud of you."

Sarah blushed. "Thank you. I want you to be proud of me, but more than that, I've learned I want to be proud of myself. I don't want to look back and regret not using this second chance at life."

"You're doing great. This baby, boy or girl, will have a great mother who'll show them the kind of person they should be."

"Thanks, Nick." Sarah rubbed her belly. "She and I wouldn't be here now if it weren't for the two of you. I know John would have killed us."

"I believe he would have, too. I'm glad you left and came to live with me."

"I'll have to go back and settle the estate. I'm selling everything and starting over. John owes us that. You said he was a wealthy man. I'll buy a little house in a nice neighborhood. Something I can maintain without help."

"There is the guest house on the property here." He nodded toward the gardens. "You could have that. Then you can keep your money for the child's wedding or education and stay home and just be a mother to her. You wouldn't have to go to work, if you didn't want to."

Annie realized that he didn't mean it as an insult, but he might as well have put a knife in her. Didn't he know she'd like nothing better than to stay home and be a mother to Evie? But she had to work. Now that her father was here, perhaps he'd take her and Evie with him. No. That would be beyond rude, to ask to barge in on their honeymoon, just so she wouldn't have to work. Besides she wanted to make her own way. If she couldn't marry Nick, she wouldn't marry anyone and she would support herself.

She'd been thinking for sometime about opening a restaurant, next to The Nugget, and then Nick wouldn't have to have one at the bar. He could make it strictly a drinking establishment. He and Blake had stopped the prostitution just after Evie was born. They told the girls they couldn't use their rooms to prostitute themselves any longer and he'd lost a few girls over that. They preferred the money they earned selling their bodies to just being saloon girls and hustling drinks.

He was making changes. Annie knew the actions were for her…hopeful that they would be enough for her to accept his proposal. But according to her father, only divesting himself of the saloon would redeem him.

The thought of the restaurant intrigued her. Would Nick invest, help her to get started? Maybe be a silent partner?

"Nick, I have a proposition I'd like to discuss with you."

"I'm all ears, sweetheart."

Annie heated at the endearment, but pushed it aside. "I'd like to open a restaurant next to The Nugget, but I'll need help getting it started. I've saved a little money but if you'd help me you could be a silent partner and I'd give you fifty percent of the profits. Then you could turn The Nugget into a strictly drinking and gaming establishment, which is what you want.

You'd be adding another business to the two you already have. What do you think? You don't have to answer now. I know that you need to discuss this with Blake first, but I hope you'll at least think about my proposal."

He set his napkin on the table. "I don't need to talk to Blake. I can help you on my own." His mouth ticked up at the corners. "I do have money that isn't tied up in our businesses."

Annie could hardly contain herself. Her heart beat a rapid tattoo and her hands grew damp.

"I'd like to open it in the vacant building next to The Nugget. Then I could still serve your customers, and also those who don't come in there because it's a saloon."

"There shouldn't be too many of those types in the area by the wharf where we're located. Mostly just sailors, rendering plant workers, some miners and a few banker types."

Annie grinned, reached over, and squeezed Nick's hand. "Thank you. You don't know how much this means to me."

He watched Annie face, grinning and glowing with happiness. "Oh, I think I do," he said quietly. He knew exactly how much it meant for her to be able to support herself. It meant everything.

"It'll take some time to get everything done. The place rented and then cleaned up. Tables and chairs, stove and icebox—all that bought and installed. Then there's the food purchases and the actual cooking. Can I put a sign in The Nugget? I'd only be open until eight at night. I want to be home for Evie. I'm sure Nellie will watch her for me…"

She rambled on. Nick knew she didn't realize that she held his hand the whole time and he wasn't about to point it out to her. He simply smiled and nodded when it was appropriate.

He looked over at Sarah and she was grinning. She could see exactly what was happening and seemed happy at what she saw.

He grinned back, then turned his attention toward Annie.

"It'll take a couple of months probably. I don't think even my father could say there was anything wrong with opening a restaurant."

Her smile faltered a little.

The bastard. He knew her enthusiasm

was dampened by thoughts of her father. Why couldn't the man just give his blessing and leave?

He and Nick definitely had to have a heart to heart. Although Nick would prefer to beat the man silly for what he'd done to Annie, he had to put those thoughts aside for her. If there was ever to be a life for them, and he was sure there would be, he needed to find a way to get along with her father. And it wasn't going to be easy.

CHAPTER 11

Two days later, Nick knocked on the hotel room door and waited for an answer. Normally he'd be sleeping after working all night, but he wanted to catch Hyrum before they left to see the sights. He didn't know for sure if Hyrum was here, but he had to start somewhere and he really didn't want to talk to her father while Annie was around.

The door opened and Hyrum Markum stood on the other side.

"May I help you, Mr. Cartwright?"

"Yes, sir. I'd like to talk to you about Annie, or...rather about us. Annie and I. I love her, Mr. Markum. I want to make her my wife. She won't marry me without your blessing. I need to know what I can do to make that happen."

"Come in, son." Hyrum stood back and let Nick pass into the room.

Doris was on the sofa doing needlepoint. "Excuse me, gentlemen. I'll go into the bedroom and leave you two to talk." She gathered her sewing into the basket at her feet and left the room.

"Sit down, please." Hyrum gestured to one of the two Queen Anne chairs that graced the sitting room.

Nick sat, waiting for the older man to speak.

Hyrum stood hands behind his back. Did the man ever not look like he was behind the pulpit when he spoke?

"I understand my daughter is also in love with you. It pains me I cannot condone her marriage. The business you run provides home to sinners. It provides sustenance to Satan's minions, liquor, gambling and women, soiled doves though they may be. I cannot in all good conscience give you my blessing."

"I've halted the prostitution. Though I was not a pimp, previously I didn't stop the girls who wanted to sell themselves. I never condoned it, but didn't do enough to stop it before. After Evie was born, I made sure it happened no more. The girls rooms are strictly off limits to the customers. The only thing I provide is liquor and gaming. I have no other form of livelihood. I'm helping Annie open a restaurant next to The Nugget and so won't be selling food any longer either."

Hyrum lifted an eyebrow. "The selling of food was the one redeeming quality that your business had. Now I cannot see that it has any."

"I won't stop Annie from her dreams. I'll do everything in my power to see that they come true. Blake and I are diversifying our businesses. We have the family emporium and The Nugget, both of which are doing quite well. Now I'll also be a silent partner in Annie's café and, given her talent, I expect her to be very successful. I'm doing my best to become the kind of man you want for your daughter."

Hyrum leaned back and crossed his legs. "Until you stop running the saloon, I don't see how you can become suitable for my Annie to marry."

Nick's ire rose and he leaned his elbows on his knees. "And what are you doing for

Annie, except crushing her dreams? You won't support her choice of a man to marry, and she's already determined she won't marry anyone she doesn't love. You won't support her financially, hence her desire to open the restaurant. Tell me, Mr. Markum, what do you do except destroy her at every opportunity?"

Hyrum stood. "I think you should leave, Mr. Cartwright. I can see we are not coming to any agreement where my daughter is concerned."

"You're right, we won't because you don't give a damn about Annie's happiness, only about your narrow beliefs."

Markum walked to the door and opened it. "Leave, Mr. Cartwright. Now."

"With pleasure." Nick walked out of the room, and the door slammed closed behind him.

Well that went well. What am I to do now? I can't stop loving Annie and I know she loves me, her father just confirmed it. But he'd rather stay in his own little world where his word is law than allow Annie to find happiness. It's no wonder he let her become a mail order bride. As long as the man was a church going man, he didn't care if Annie was happy or not. There's got to be something I can do.

*****

Annie thought Nick arranged for a lease on the building next to The Nugget, but instead he bought it outright.

She paced in front of the door out of Nick's office. "You didn't have to do that. What if I don't succeed? You'll be stuck with another building."

Nick sat behind his desk. "That won't happen. But if it did, we'd simply expand The Nugget into it."

She bit her bottom lip. "Well, if you're sure."

"Annie."

"Yes?"

"Come here."

She walked over to the desk.

"Around here." He moved back his chair.

After a moment's pause, she rounded the desk and stood in front of him.

He patted his lap.

Her eyes widened and she shook her head.

He smiled, nodded and patted his lap again.

Annie sighed, sat and put her arms around his neck. "This is highly improper."

"Everything about us is highly improper." He wrapped his arms around her and anchored her safely on his lap. "Now, listen to me. You are not going to fail. You are too stubborn to do so." He rolled his eyes and looked toward the ceiling. "Believe me I know just how stubborn you can be."

"I'm just nervous."

"Well, until I can procure all the equipment, you don't have any reason to be nervous. Everything will remain as it is. You'll work here, I'll play with Evie and we'll both try to convince your father to let us marry. I almost told him I'd ruined you, so he'd have to let us marry."

Annie sucked in a breath. "Nick!"

"I didn't but I'm still tempted. If I thought you'd go along with it, I'd still do it in a heartbeat. I'll do almost anything to marry you. And I know you love me."

"I don't." She stiffened and pulled away.

He didn't loosen his hold but gently brought her back. "You do. Your father told me you did. He said it pained him to turn me down because you loved me."

"It doesn't matter if I do. He'll never

agree."

"Annie. You're a woman, fully grown and a mother besides. You can do what you want. You can do what's best for Evie, and you know I'm best for Evie."

"I know," she whispered and laid her head on Nick's shoulder.

"I'll find an answer, Annie. I promise."

*****

February 22, 1869

Across town at the home of Seth and Louisa Christenson
Partner to William White in White & Christenson,
Import and Export

Louisa Christenson sat across the breakfast table listening to her husband Seth jabber on about something. She took a bite of her toast, sipped her tea and mostly ignored him.

"The ship is on its way. It stopped in Los Angeles and will be here the end of the week. Think of it Louisa. We'll be rich, able to pay off the rest of our creditors and have money left over. I sent a letter to Annie to let her know. This will be a load off of her mind. William left her in such dire straits and because I had almost everything in the ship as well, I couldn't help her. I've always felt a bit guilty about that."

Rich? Did he say rich? She shook her head to clear it before steam blew from her ears.

As usual, Seth was totally unaware of Louisa's anger or he ignored it, which was worse in her mind.

Covering her ire, she said sweetly. "Where is Annie now? I thought she would have gone back to New York when William died and left her penniless."

"No. She stayed in San Francisco. She had a baby, Evangeline, just a month after William died. The child must be about nine months old by now."

"But if she was penniless, how did she stay in San Francisco?"

"She went to live with Blake and Nellie Malone. She and Nellie are fast friends since they both came here as mail order brides."

"And you told her the ship was found and is on its way?" Her voice was as steady as she could make it, when she really wanted to scream at him.

"Of course. Half of the ship is hers. She'll be a very wealthy woman now. She can quit working as a cook at that saloon."

"How do you know all of this?"

"We've kept in touch since William

passed. I contacted her once a month to let her know if there had been any news about the ship, and just to see if she is well. I was always hopeful that the ship would be found. And look, I was right."

"Yes, you were."

Louisa Christenson stared at her husband. They could have had it all. Stupid man. *He* didn't know what he'd done. But Louisa did. He'd signed his death warrant. She wanted it all and there was no way she'd let him or Annie White stop her. The ship was hers. Alone.

*****

"There's a letter for you." Nellie crossed the parlor to the settee where Annie sat with her crochet. She watched Evie walk around the table, bouncing every few steps delighted with herself. Daniel, was usually right behind her, they were only two weeks apart after all, but today he was content to play with his toys on a blanket.

Nellie handed her the envelope.

Annie ran her finger under the seal and read.

My dear Annie,
I'm writing to let you know
that the ship we thought lost

has finally been found. It has docked at the port in Los Angeles. You're rich, Annie. I know that William left you in a financial bind and I'm glad to be able to tell you that it is finally over.

The ship is called the Windflower, and will be docking in San Francisco on Monday or Tuesday of next week at pier six.

Forever your friend,
Seth Christenson

"N...Nellie," Annie's voice wavered. "Nellie. The ship. it's coming."

"The ship? What ship?" Nellie sat forward in the chair opposite the settee.

"William's ship. The one we thought lost." Annie blinked hard. "I'll be rich, Nellie. William had everything in that ship. That's why I had to sell almost all our belongings when he died. Now, I won't need Nick to help me with the restaurant. I can afford to do it on my own if I decide to continue with the plan. I have options now that I didn't have before."

Nellie stood, picked up Evie who had fallen, and put her over on the blanket with Daniel to play. "Annie, take some time before you make any decisions. What does this mean for you and Nick?"

"Don't you see? Nick can sell the saloon. We can get married. Between the two of us, we'll have all the money we'll need, and he could take over William's business. Until now there wasn't any business to take over. Seth kept whatever was left going, but now…"

Nellie frowned. "That's making a lot of assumptions. What if Nick doesn't want to go into the shipping business? The Nugget has been very good to both Nick and Blake."

Annie shook her head. "All I know is that Williams partner, Seth Christenson, was Nick's best friend when they were young, before Nick met Blake. But for some reason they had a falling out about six years ago."

Nodding Nellie said, "Ah, I wondered why Nick hadn't mentioned it before. It would have killed him to see you with William, or whenever he saw his friend. But if they had a falling out, don't you think that might give him pause to work with the man?"

"We didn't see each other. William and I didn't see Seth and his wife, Louisa, on a social basis. According to William, she didn't think I was good enough to be her friend." Annie pursed her lips, "That was fine with me. The few times I did visit with her, she was so uppity I didn't want to get to know her any better. As to Nick working with Seth, I honestly hadn't thought about it."

"This money will mean the world to you and to Nick. But it sounds like there are a lot of things you haven't thought about. You need to talk to Nick before you make any plans."

"You're right." Annie bounced in her seat, unable to sit still or get the grin off her face. "I'm just so excited because I can finally see Nick and I being together."

Nellie sat next to Annie and took one of her hands. "Honey, money was never what was keeping you apart and you know it. Your father and your beliefs are keeping you apart."

Annie sighed, some of the excitement of the moment leaving her. "And those haven't changed."

"Oh, I think they have. You know now

that people who work in a saloon and most of those who use them are good people, just trying to get by until the next sunrise."

"You're right. I have changed, but my father hasn't. Unless Nick sells the saloon, there is no way Father will ever give his blessing."

"Did you have his blessing to marry William?"

"Yes. William appeared to be an upstanding man and he *was* a church goer. Father even wrote to his reverend before agreeing to let me go."

Nellie continued to hold Annie's hand in hers. "But you didn't love William and he didn't treat you well. He preferred his business to you. That proves that just because one attends church doesn't mean they are a good man. William wasn't but Nick is."

Annie took her hand from Nellie's and looked down at her hands, turning them over to see the scars on her left hand. She'd taken off her wedding ring the day after William's funeral. She'd kept it, not because it meant anything to her, but because she didn't know if she might need to pawn it in order to survive, but she'd never worn the gaudy thing since he died. It had a large diamond surrounded by many smaller baguette diamonds and was probably worth a small fortune. It had been her emergency fund. What she'd have had to use if not for Nellie and Blake taking her in.

She kept the ring thinking maybe to sell it when Evie got older to pay for her wedding. She wanted Evie to have the wedding Annie didn't get. With flowers and a party afterward. Dancing and music. And a beautiful dress that she could pass down to her daughters.

The ring would pay for that. As far as Annie was concerned, it wasn't good for anything else. She even found out that Louisa Christenson had helped William pick it out. Annie should have known. The jewelry was exactly Louisa's style. Tacky and expensive.

"You're right about all of it. I'll give it more thought but I will talk to Nick. If he'd let it, this could be the answer to everything for us."

CHAPTER 12

Annie remembered her excitement about the ship. She hadn't talked to Nick yet. There hadn't been time, she'd had to start cooking as soon as she arrived at The Nugget. Tonight was the most popular of her menus—steak fingers. She finally finished preparing the fingers and walked out of the kitchen to change the sandwich board with the new offering. Rounding the bar, she heard a commotion just in front of her.

"Give me the money in the drawer, old man."

"Sam?" said Annie.

"Annie, get back!" shouted Sam.

"Annie?" asked the man. "Annie White?"

"Yes," she replied, frozen in spot,

confused how a stranger knew her name.

The gunman turned toward her. Just as he fired Sam hit his arm with the bat he kept behind the bar. The shot went off target.

Something slammed her off her feet and she hit the floor, her head bouncing off the wood. Pain screamed through her mind, and then she was still.

Nick opened the door to his office and ran out gun in hand. The sound of the gunshot rang in his ears. He looked over the railing to the bar below and saw a man fleeing from the scene. The patrons got out of his way, and he would have made a quick escape if he hadn't collided with Blake coming in the door.

"Do you have him?" Nick called to Blake.

Several customers came to Blake's aid, once the gunman was down. They kicked and beat him until the man was bloodied.

"Stop!" yelled Blake before the men killed the fugitive. He looked up at Nick. "We got him." He held out his arms.

Nick glanced over the room and down at the bar. Several of the girls were gathered at the end of the long slab of polished mahogany. Sally Jo looked up and saw him.

"Nick," she called. "It's Annie."

Heart pounding he ran along the walkway and down the stairs. When he reached the crowd of women he stopped.

"Move. Let me through."

He reached Annie and knelt next to her. Blood ran from a wound on her head.

"Sam, send for the doctor."

Nick gathered her into his arms and carried her up to his office. He laid her on the settee, and then took the handkerchief from his pocket. He poured some water from the pitcher on the cabinet behind his desk, then knelt next to the sofa and dabbed at her injury. Once he got the blood removed, he saw a wound on the right side of her forehead, and a lump forming the left.

"Annie. Honey. Wake up."

This was his fault. He never should have let her work here. It was too dangerous a place. For Sarah, too. Maybe Annie's father was right. Saloons were the devil's workshop. It certainly looked like it right now as he watched Annie's still form. He knew he wasn't thinking straight, it didn't matter. The only thing that mattered now was the beautiful woman lying still on his settee.

"Annie mine, wake up, please. I promise if you'll just wake up, I'll make sure you stay safe."

The only way he could do that was to make sure he stayed as far away from her as possible. He wasn't worthy of someone like Annie. She was so sweet and good. And what about Evie? How could he be a good father to her when he ran a saloon? He couldn't do that. Not to either of them. He'd have to cut all ties to them both. It was the only way. He loved them too much to put them in any kind of danger.

Rap! Rap! Rap!

Nick stood and went to the door. Sally Jo was there with Doc Robertson. His office was only a few blocks down from The Nugget. He was the one who got called for anything that needed a doctor—from gunshot wounds to one of the girls with a cold.

"What happened to her, Nick?"

"I don't know. She may have been shot, but I can't find any bullet wounds, except a graze on her head."

"Let me examine her."

The doctor examined Annie for bullet holes or other wounds. He watched as the doctor ran his fingers over her head.

"She's got this," the doctor pointed at the wound that was bleeding. "And the lump on the other side. I think she must have hit the floor hard when the bullet hit her. Now we wait until she wakes up."

"How long will that take?" asked Nick, who never raised his gaze from Annie.

"I don't know. She's suffered a concussion, and could wake in minutes, or…"

Nick clenched his jaw and his fist "There is no 'or'. She *will* wake up. What can I do?"

"There's not much. Make sure she stays warm. Give her liquids if you can get her to drink them. Use a washcloth to dribble it into her mouth if you need to."

Nick nodded. "Thanks, Doc. I'll take her home now. Blake and Nellie will be more than capable of taking care of her." *I need to stay as far away as possible.*

He bundled Annie into a blanket he kept on the end of the settee for when he slept at the office. He used to do that a lot before Annie. Once he was sure that she was as comfortable as he could make her, he carried her to his carriage. He held her tight in his arms knowing it would be the last time.

"Annie, please wake up. I'll do anything. Please."

They arrived at Blake's home in less than thirty minutes, though it seemed too long for her to still be unconscious and not long enough for him to hold her.

He got up to the front door and kicked it, trying to jostle her as little as possible.

The door opened, and James, the Malone's butler, stood there.

"Mr. Cartwright, come in. Mrs. White? Is she all right?"

"No, she's not, get Mrs. Malone right away. I'll take Annie to her room."

"Yes, sir."

James hurried away, practically running down the hall.

Nick took the stairs two at a time. He heard Nellie running up the stairs behind him. When he got to Annie's room he had to wait for Nellie to open the door and then go inside and turn down the blankets before he could lay Annie on the bed.

"What happened?" asked Nellie.

"There was a shooting, and Annie was grazed by a bullet. But the doctor's more worried about the lump on her head."

"Is Blake all right?" Nellie's voice betrayed her fear for her husband.

"Yes, he's fine. He and some of the customers apprehended the man when he tried to escape. More's the pity, he's probably in police custody by now."

"Why is that bad?"

"Because I want to beat him with my bare hands for what he did to her."

He stood by the bed and held Annie's hand.

"This is my fault. I should never have given her the job. I should just have given her the money and let her go back to her father."

Nellie put her hand on Nick's shoulder. "She didn't want the money. I'm not sure she wants to go back to her father at all, she just felt she didn't have another choice."

"I would have married her, you know that."

"Would have? Have you given up trying to woo her?"

"Yes. She deserves so much more than I can give her. I won't bring her down to my level. Her father is right."

"Nick." Nellie moved her hand to his arm. "This is not your fault, and her father is wrong. About Blake and about you. Even Reverend Schossow is coming around to believing that Blake and I are good people. It just takes time."

"I don't have time."

"But what about the ship?" said Nellie. "The proceeds from the sale of the goods on the ship can give you all the time you need."

He cocked his head and furrowed his brow. "What ship?"

"Didn't you and Annie talk?"

"Not tonight. There wasn't time. She started cooking and I had to see to payroll."

"Oh, dear." She took Nick by the arm. "Please don't make any decisions until you talk to Annie."

He frowned. "I don't know that it will make any difference, but I'll wait."

"Promise?"

He patted her hand on his arm. "I promise."

*****

Annie awoke, cringed, and closed her eyes again. The light caused her pain, she turned away, and the movement caused her more pain. She moaned and put her hand against her head hoping, to ease the torment.

"Annie? Honey, look at me."

As much as she didn't want to open her eyes, she wanted to see him more. "Nick? What happened?"

"You were shot. It's my fault. I never should have let you work at The Nugget."

"Shot?" She tried to sit up but pain and nausea forced her back down. "Sam? Is he all right?"

"Yes. He's fine. When the man shot you, it must have scared him because he turned and ran."

Memories flooded her thoughts. "He said my name before he turned and shot me. If Sam hadn't hit his arm with that bat, I'd be dead. Nick, I think he was sent to kill me."

"Why would anyone want to kill you?"

"I don't know." Annie sighed and closed her eyes again. "Please close the drapes."

Nick let go of her hand, and she felt the room darken. She opened her eyes again and this time there was only a little pain.

"Thank you. Where am I?"

"You're at Blake and Nellie's."

She nodded. The slight movement sent a lightning bolt through her head. "How long have I been here?"

Nick sat in a chair next to the bed. "It's

morning. You've been unconscious for most of the night."

"Why did you stay? What about The Nugget?"

"I didn't want Nellie to have to stay up with you. She's got the two babies to look after and needed her rest. Blake is at The Nugget."

"Evie?" Annie again tried to rise, but Nick put his hand on her shoulder and gently pushed her back. "Is Evie okay?"

"She's fine. Nellie is taking good care of her."

Her eyes filled with tears. *Things are going to change.* "I'm a terrible mother. I should be taking care of my daughter. Well, now I'll be able to."

"Then you're not coming back to the saloon."

"No. Flossie will have to do the cooking."

"That's not a problem."

"Nick."

"Yes."

"The ship came in." She grinned and watched his face for a reaction.

"The ship?" His eyes rounded. "You mean William's ship? The one they thought lost at sea?"

"Yes. It was caught in a hurricane and then had to put into port to repair damages, but it's in and according to Seth, the cargo is even richer than they thought it would be."

Annie closed her eyes and rested back against the pillows but not before she saw him stiffen.

"That's wonderful for you...and Seth."

At the tightness in his voice, she opened her eyes. "What happened between you and Seth?"

He fisted his hands and spoke through clenched teeth. "He married Louisa is what happened."

"I've no love for the woman but you appear to have genuine hate."

Nick looked away from her. "She got me drunk and slept with me, then tried to tell me that I was the father of the child she was expecting."

I don't really want to hear this, but I need to understand. "You didn't believe that?"

"No. I only slept with her that once and I'm not sure we even had sex. She was pregnant with someone else's child. Maybe Seth's, maybe not, but she made him believe it was his when I didn't fall for her scheme. I told him what she'd try to do to me. His response was to belt me, nearly breaking my jaw and marry her anyway. We haven't spoken since."

"I see."

"What do you see?"

"You wouldn't want to take over William's business then because it would mean working with Seth."

"No, I wouldn't want to take over William's business." He shook his head and narrowed his eyes. "Why would you ask me that?"

"I just thought now that the ship is in, the business will be more profitable than ever and I need someone there to watch out for my interests…and…and"

"And what? Say what you're thinking Annie."

She hears the anger in his voice.

"I'm thinking my head hurts and I really don't want to be talking about this right now."

"Of course." Nick dipped his head for a moment and then took her hand. "I'm sorry, sweetheart. I shouldn't be pressing you when you've just been through such a traumatic event."

"I need to rest. Please tell me that you'll be here when I awake."

"Annie, I'm not the man for you. What I do…it put you in danger…more than once."

Annie's eyes widened, then her brows furrowed and tears welled in her eyes. "I'm starting to make the choices for my life. Don't give up now, Nick. Please. Be here when I wake up."

"All right. I'll be here."

*****

Annie awoke in the dark. Definitely night. Gingerly she sat up waiting for the lightning strike and the nausea. There was only a dull ache and some dizziness. Not too bad. She lit the lamp on her bedside table and went into the bathroom to examine herself in the mirror.

The bandage around her head covered the right temple where she knew, from talking to Nick, a bullet had grazed her. Both of her eyes were black and blue, which surprised her. On the left side of her head, just above her temple was a lump the size of a chicken egg. She must have hit the floor very hard. The lump was what had alarmed the doctor so much. She reached up and gently touched the protrusion. The pain was immediate. *Okay, I won't do that again.*

On her way back to the bedroom she stopped by Evie's crib. She needed to see her little girl and assure herself she was all right. The crib was empty.

"Evie," she whispered and headed for the Malone nursery.

She opened the door and saw Nellie in the rocking chair, holding Daniel and softly singing.

"Come in," said Nellie, giving her a gentle smile. "I wondered when you'd be awake."

"I woke just a short while ago." She braced her hand on the wall for a moment before moving forward. "I just want to look at Evie for a little while, I panicked a little when I found her crib empty, then I thought you might have moved her in here. But why not bring her crib?"

"We'll need a third crib in a few months and decided to get it now and let Evie use it. We moved her here to be with Daniel at night. It was much easier for me and she wasn't alone."

"I wasn't complaining. I'm glad you thought of it. I'm such a terrible mother.

Evie is so lucky to have you. Did you just tell me, in a roundabout way, that you're expecting?" Annie crossed the room and sat in the second rocker next to Nellie. In a thoughtful gesture they had two in place so both Annie and Nellie could rock their children to sleep. Or Violet could sit next to Nellie while she fed Daniel, and talk a mile a minute. The thought made Annie smile.

Nellie laughed softly. "Yes, I did. And you're not a terrible mother."

They both whispered, so as not to wake the children. Violet was also in the room, and if she woke, no one would get back to sleep. The child was a force of nature when she was awake.

"Congratulations on the new baby."

"Thanks. With the new one coming, I'll soon wean Daniel."

"It's time I weaned Evie, too. She's always hungry for more than milk anyway."

"I know," said Nellie with a laugh.

"You wouldn't have to know if I wasn't letting you raise my daughter. I'm surprised Evie knows who I am lately."

"That's ridiculous and anyway your situation is about to change. You don't have to work at The Nugget or anywhere else now."

Frowning, Annie nodded. "I told Nick I wasn't going back and Flossie will have to do the cooking. I told him about the ship, too. You were right. He doesn't want to take William's place in the business. I'll either have to trust that Seth is running the business with both of our interests in mind or work there myself."

Nellie shook her head. "You can't do that. You just said you want to be a mother to Evie."

"Well, what else can I do?" she said in frustration. "Someone has to watch out for our interests, Evie's and mine."

"Let me talk to Blake about it. Maybe you can hire someone. He'd know if that's a possibility."

Annie looked at Daniel, sleeping soundly in his mother's arms. "Daniel is asleep now. You can go back to bed."

"I will if you will. Evie is asleep, too."

She looked in the crib at her sleeping child and smiled. "She's growing so fast and I feel like I'm missing it."

"You're not missing it. You're still here for her every day. You care for her, nurse her, play with her and still manage to go to work every night. I don't know how you do it. You've got to be exhausted."

Annie got up, took one last look at Evie, and walked to the door where Nellie waited.

"I *am* tired. There is no doubt about that. Sometimes all I want to do is sleep. But I know I can't so I go on about my business. I've done all of this, working to make a living, for Evie. For us. I can't continue to live off of your goodness. You know it and so do I. Now I have options. There's light where there was only darkness before."

Nellie cocked her head and frowned. "You know you can stay here as long as you need. You're not taking up any space, we have four empty bedrooms as well as the suite you're in and another suite besides. Trust me, when I say having you here is no trouble. And I love having another woman to talk to."

They walked down the hall toward Annie's room. Feeling a sudden chill, Annie gathered her lacy robe closer to her neck. Why she hadn't worn her flannel robe, she didn't know. There was certainly no one to impress.

"But you have all those society women you visit with," said Annie.

"None of them are really my friends. I can't tell them my problems or share my dreams, like I can with you. I know that I can tell you anything and you won't judge me for it."

"I feel the same about you." Annie opened the door to her room. "Come in, just for a minute."

"You really need your rest. Believe it or not, you've been through a traumatic experience."

Annie chuckled and then groaned and raised a hand to her cheek. "God, that hurts. Who knew getting barely shot was so painful."

"I think it's that goose egg on the other side that is giving you the pain."

Annie walked to her bed and sat back, pulling up her knees. "Sit down, Nellie. Relax a bit. I know you don't get much more rest than I do, especially with two babies to take care of."

Nellie sat on the edge of the bed. "Ah, but I have Blake to help me. When you're working and both babies need attention, I have Blake take Daniel and I take Evie. The arrangement works out very well. And for the most part the babies entertain each other.

So unless they need feeding or changing, we don't have to do much."

"I know you're just saying those things to make me feel better."

"I'm not." Nellie leaned forward and took Annie's hand. "It's true. Having Evie here has been wonderful for all of us and especially for Daniel. I like to think it's been good for Evie, too."

"You know it has." Annie smiled and leaned back on the pillows, stacked against the headboard. "I think I'm just feeling sorry for myself."

"You're allowed. The past couple of months have been difficult, what with Sarah's husband trying to kill her, Nick getting stabbed, your burned hands, and now this. No wonder Nick says working at The Nugget is too dangerous."

"Well, now he won't have to worry about it." Her eyes filled with tears she wouldn't let fall. "I'll miss seeing him every day."

"Marry him and that won't be a problem."

Annie shook her head and sniffled. "As you said, things haven't really changed. Money was never the problem."

Nellie took a deep breath. "You'll have to decide what is more important to you: your father's beliefs, or Nick. I know you don't believe the same as your father does. Not anymore. You've come to know the people by who they are and not by just what they do."

"You're right. But I want my father to give us his blessing. I need his blessing. I've tried all my life to please him and make him proud of me. I need him to be a part of my life, of Evie's life."

"So instead of being with Nick every day, someone who loves you and loves Evie, you would turn all that down to have the blessing of a man you will only see once or twice a year, if that? Think about *what* you're doing, Annie."

Annie closed her eyes. Sadness and clarity flowed through her. When put like that, giving up Nick didn't make sense. Her father was going on a trip around the world with Doris. She wouldn't see him for at least two years after he left San Francisco. Was she really willing to give up Nick, give up love and family for an outdated belief held by her father? A belief she no longer shared?

She opened her eyes, maybe for the first

time. "You're right, Nellie. I will ask Nick to marry me."

"That's my girl. Now get some sleep. I have a feeling you'll have wonderful dreams."

Nellie stood, then leaned down and gave Annie a kiss in the middle of her forehead, between her two injuries.

"Thank you for helping me to see the truth of things. I've been so stubborn, so wrong. Nick is a good man and," Annie laughed, barely more than a little chuckle. "He's going to get me...if he still wants me."

Nellie smiled and left the room.

Annie was more awake than ever. How would ask Nick to marry her? What if he said, no?

CHAPTER 13

Nick wasn't usually up so early, but today was important. He walked into Blake's library, unannounced.

Blake looked up from his desk, where he sat in shirtsleeves working on his accounts. "Nick. What brings you by so early this morning?"

"I promised Annie I'd be here."

"Ah, that explains why you're wearing your best suit. I didn't think it was to see me."

Nick pulled at the jet black cravat perfectly tied at his throat. He paced the room in front of Blake's massive mahogany desk. "I'm asking her again, for the last time, to marry me. Did she tell you

William's ship came in? She's rich now, Blake. She doesn't need to marry me."

"Did you think she needed to marry you before? Is that why you asked her?"

He stopped and dropped into the chair facing Blake. "No, of course not. I asked her because I love her."

"And that has changed? That's why you're giving up if she doesn't say yes? You won't love her anymore?"

Nick sat on the edge of the chair, anger flowed through him and something else. Fear. "I'll always love her. Are you trying to make me angry?"

"No, I'm trying to make you open your eyes and see. Annie was raised solely by her father after her mother died. She's close to him, even when he's not physically here. Is it any wonder she wants his blessing?"

Nick settled back into the chair. "I suppose not."

Blake steepled his hands, elbows resting on the desk. "So how will you convince her to marry you without that blessing?"

"I don't know. She's just got to say yes. I don't know what I'll do without her."

Blake leaned back in his chair and crossed his legs. Then he began to twirl the pencil in his hand. "Or you could sell me your half of The Nugget and concentrate on the amusement park. It's gotten so popular we need to expand and I want to build a boardwalk. You could concentrate your efforts there."

"Or," Nick said with a sigh. "I could take William's place in the import/export business, like Annie wants me to."

Blake stopped twirling the pencil and leaned forward. "And you said?"

Nick let out a breath and leaned back in the chair. "No."

"Why? That would be the perfect solution. You could protect Annie's interests and get out of the saloon business. Why on earth would you say no?"

"Seth Christenson."

"What does Seth Christenson have to do with this?

"He is…was William's business partner."

Frustration tinged Blake's voice. "Continue, please."

"Suffice it to say that Seth and I were once good friends, until he met Louisa. She's a vicious, lying bitch and when I tried to tell Seth that, he belted me and married her anyway. We haven't spoken since."

"How long ago was that?"

"Six years ago. She tried to convince me the baby she carried was mine."

"Could it have been?"

Nick didn't like talking about the past. He stood, placed his hands on Blake's desk and leaned forward. "No. Never. She got me drunk and we may have slept together but I doubt seriously that we had sex. I was too inebriated to have performed anything but a swan dive onto my pillow."

Blake nodded. "Ah. Oldest trick in the book."

"Yes, and I tried to tell Seth that, but he wouldn't listen. I'm telling you, Blake, that woman is evil, right down to the core. I don't want Annie anywhere near her."

"All the more reason for you to take over for William, so Annie doesn't have to."

"Why would Annie need to take over for William? Seth will see that she's paid fairly for her share."

"Will he?" Blake leaned forward and rested his forearm on the desk. "What about Louisa? Will she want to see Annie taken care of fairly?"

"I see what you mean." Nick ran his

hands through his hair and began pacing again. "Sounds like I don't have much choice, if I want to protect Annie."

"If you really love her, then you know it's the right thing to do."

"I do love her. I'd do anything for her, and I guess now is the time I should prove it. She means more to me than The Nugget, or anything else."

"Good. Go tell her."

Nick walked to the door. Then he turned back to Blake. "Thanks for steering me in the right direction."

"Anytime. I know how much the right woman is worth. She's more precious than gold."

Nick knew the smile on Blake's face was one of supreme satisfaction, and was put there by Nellie. Nick wanted to feel that same sense of contentment, and Annie was the only one who could give that to him.

He walked upstairs to Annie's room. She was still in bed recovering from her wounds. Wounds he was responsible for. He didn't pull the trigger, but it was his fault nonetheless. If not for him she wouldn't have been there. Wouldn't have been in danger. The more he thought about it, there was no way he could ask her to marry him. He'd told Blake he would, but no way would he bring her down to his level. He knocked on the door.

"Come in," came her sweet voice from the other side.

"Hello. Are you decent?"

"I am. Come in, please."

Nick walked to her bed, bent and gave her a gentle kiss on the cheek. "How are you feeling?"

"I'm fine."

He sat in the chair next to the bed. "You're not fine. You're wounded and it's my fault."

"No, Nick. It's not and we're not going through this again. I'm not returning to The Nugget, so you have no worries."

"I suppose."

"Have you thought any more about my offer for you to take over the position in William's company?"

Nick took her hand. It was so small in his. How could he make her give up her beliefs for him? If she married him, she'd be giving up everything. He couldn't ask that of her.

"I have. I'll take the job in the business.

I don't want you to have to worry about anything."

"Good. Thank you."

"You're welcome."

She looked up at him with those wide blue eyes of hers, and he was almost lost. Almost gave into the longings of his heart. He'd give her the moon if she asked. He needed to leave, needed to be strong. Evie. He'd go see his baby girl. She always made his day better.

"Nick, I…"

He stood abruptly. "I need to get back to work, but I want to see Evie before I go."

"All right. Will I see you later?"

"I don't know. The night is going to be a late one. I have to get someone trained to take over management of The Nugget, so I might not be by for a few days or so."

She nodded. He saw in her eyes that she was disappointed, but better now than later. He'd work for her, see her safe, but that was all. She was still too good for the likes of him, even if he didn't own a saloon.

*****

Annie watched Nick's broad shoulders disappear through her bedroom door out into the hall. Tears formed in her eyes and she felt one trail its way down her cheek. She hadn't had a chance to ask him to marry her. He looked like he couldn't wait to get away from her. Something had happened. Maybe he finally got tired of her saying no.

At least he still wanted to see Evie. That didn't seem to have changed. She wasn't giving up. Nick was the most important person in her life, next to Evie, and it was time he knew it. If she wasn't feeling so bad and crying, she'd follow him to the nursery, but right now, she only wanted to lay here and cry. Tears for her pain and for perhaps losing Nick to her foolish pride.

*****

Annie sat in the window seat, watching the fog roll down the hill from Marin and right into the bay. From the Malone house, high on Russian Hill seeing the bay was easy. The fog rolling in was almost daily occurrence, one Annie never tired of seeing.

Almost two weeks had passed since Nick had come to see her. She hadn't seen him since. He seemed to be avoiding her and was doing a very good job of it. If he needed to see Blake about The Nugget, he'd go see him at the amusement park.

He'd taken William's position at White

and Christenson Importers but that still didn't mean he saw her. If he needed her thoughts on anything, he sent a letter by messenger and the boy always waited for a response, so there was no excuse for Annie to visit the office. She couldn't have until now anyway. Her wounds kept her from leaving the house.

Blake told her that Seth and Nick had reconciled. Both realized that they were wrong to have expected the other to feel the same way. He told Blake he thought that Seth had realized, at least in part, that Nick had been right about Louisa. Seth knew now she wasn't the delicate flower she'd appeared to be six years ago.

Annie was glad they were friends again and that Nick was happy or at least appeared to be. She knew she and Evie weren't. He hadn't even been by to see her baby girl, possibly afraid he'd run into Annie or he had simply removed himself from their lives.

Well, there was something Annie could do about that. He may not want to see her, but she'd be damned if he just disappeared from Evie's life without an explanation. Her baby was miserable and she intended to find out why.

*****

Louisa stirred the tea and smiled at her husband. She'd put arsenic in it as she'd been doing for the last couple of weeks, and he was very sick now. By the time he finished this cup, she hoped he'd be dead. She was tired of watching him die and was ready for the deed to be done. Then there was only one thing between her and the riches on the ship. Annie White. She would have to die, too. Not that Louisa minded, she'd discovered she had a taste for *elimination.* She'd already hired a man to kill Annie, but he'd failed and gotten caught in the attempt. Luckily for Louisa, he'd believed her when she'd told him she'd have his family killed if he talked. He hadn't given her up.

After she had the money, maybe she'd be rich enough to change Nick Cartwright's mind about her. She'd been wrong to try and foist off the child she carried as his but she'd wanted him so much and he wouldn't give her the time of day. In more ways than one, she'd been desperate.

Seth had believed her, of course. He was in love with her; he'd have believed anything she said. The possibility that

Louisa might have lied, never occurred to him.

She wasn't really sure who Frankie's father was. It could have been one of the two married men she was seeing at the time. The only thing she was sure about Frankie's sire was that he was *not* Seth Christenson. He didn't know that, though. Frankie looked like Louisa, with blond hair and blue eyes, so passing him off as Seth's son was easy. And Seth doted on him, as did Louisa. He was the one thing they never fought about.

Most women would consider themselves lucky. Seth was a good man, husband, and father. Louisa should be happy, but she wanted more. No, not just more. She wanted it all.

*****

Annie got the news by messenger. She thanked the boy and gave him a quarter. She kept several in a bowl on the hall table, just for the messengers, who came on almost a daily basis. If nothing else, Nick was determined to keep her informed of everything that happened at the company.

> *Annie,*
> *Seth   Christenson   has*

passed away. He had been sick, with what they now think was the flu, very nearly since I came to work here. Louisa found him dead in their bed this morning.

The funeral is Thursday morning, ten o'clock at Chapel of our Lady church on Moraga Avenue at the Presidio. Seth was a former Naval Officer and will have a military funeral with honors.

Nick

She gasped. Dead? Seth? But he was such a young man. Only thirty or so. Nick's age. She hurried to find Nellie in the parlor.

"Seth is dead," she told her friend.

Nellie set her needlepoint in her lap. "Your business partner?"

Annie nodded. "I just received this from Nick." She handed her the note.

"Well," said Nellie as she scanned the paper. "Nick will have to see you at the funeral. He can't avoid attending."

Annie perked up and then immediately felt guilty. "He can't avoid me then, can he?"

"I don't see how."

"I don't have anything appropriate to wear. I got rid of all my black dresses."

"I'd give you something, but Blake won't let me wear black dresses unless it's an evening gown. You remember. When I first got here, I only had three ensembles that weren't black because I'd been in mourning for more than two years, thanks to my mother-in-law who refused for us to wear anything else."

"I'll just have to wear my purple dress. It's the darkest I have."

"It also is one of your most flattering, which I'm sure has nothing to do with anything."

"I have to honor my business partner the best way I can."

"Yes, you do," agreed Nellie. "But, with the way Nick has been behaving, the service will be your only chance for to see him."

"I know and I want him to miss me. I want him to regret staying away. Will you keep Evie?"

"Certainly. You don't need to ask."

"Thank you. I better go make sure my dress is pressed and ready to go."

Annie walked out, smiling...happy for

the first time in weeks and guilty at the same time. She was sad Seth was gone and yet extremely grateful to him, too. She'd get to see Nick and make him talk to her. She knew it might be her last chance.

CHAPTER 14

Blake escorted bAnnie to the funeral, while Nellie stayed home with the children. Annie hoped that, since Blake was with her, Nick might come by and talk to them, rather than her having to approach him. They pulled up to the small white church with the cross on top and the carriage stopped.

Blake hopped out and then held his hand for Annie.

"Come on, Annie, take my hand," Blake coaxed.

She was suddenly afraid to see Nick. What if he rejected her? Taking a deep breath she accepted Blake's outstretched hand.

"Thank you. I find I'm afraid."

"Nick won't bite."

She smiled. "Are you sure about that?"

He grinned. "I'm pretty sure. Unless you want him to, of course."

She laughed and stepped out of the gleaming black carriage. Once on the ground, she ran her hands down the front of her dress, straightening wrinkles. As planned, she'd worn the purple silk trimmed with pleated satin and a satin rosette at the top of the placket hiding the buttons.

"Stop stalling. You look lovely."

She sighed. "All right, I'm ready."

"It'll be fine. You'll see." He tucked her hand into the crook of his elbow and they walked into the church together.

The event wasn't fine. Nick was there with the widow, Louisa Christenson. She held Nick's arm in a death grip and acted like they were a couple rather than him just being her escort for her husband's funeral. And she was dressed more for a ball than a funeral. Her dress was black silk, off the shoulder, but had the entire upper bodice and shoulder filled with black lace so it technically wasn't a ball gown, but it was definitely alluring.

Nick didn't seem impressed, much to

Annie's delight.

Annie and Blake approached them. "Hello, Louisa. I'm so sorry for your loss."

"Thank you, Annie. First William, and now my poor Seth. Makes you wonder if our business is cursed."

"Don't be ridiculous, Louisa," said Nick, frowning. "You'd have me dying next."

"Oh, no, we can't have that, now can we?" She patted his hand. "Don't you agree, Annie?"

For a moment, Annie was silent, drinking in the sight of Nick, resplendent in his black suit, with vest and hip-length jacket. He held his top hat in the hand not caught in Louisa's death grip. He eschewed the popular mutton-chop sideburns for ones that hit even with his earlobe. He looked more handsome than ever.

"Annie? Are you all right?" asked Nick, his deep voice washing over her like an ocean wave.

Shaking her head, she came out of her reverie. "Yes, I'm fine. No, you're right Louisa," she said without taking her gaze off Nick. "We certainly don't want Nick dying. That would be just too coincidental."

She glanced at Louisa but ignored the

cold stare she received from the woman.

"Blake Malone. You remember Louisa Christenson," said Nick.

"Of course." Blake took her outstretched hand and shook it. "You have my deepest sympathy for your loss, Mrs. Christenson."

Louisa sniffed loudly. "Thank you, Mr. Malone. I appreciate the thought very much."

"Had Seth been ill for long?" asked Annie.

"No, not long at all. A couple of weeks. His death was totally unexpected," answered Louisa, followed by a sniffle into her handkerchief.

Something about the way Louisa said the words made Annie uneasy. There was more to this story than Louisa was saying.

Blake took Louisa's arm and tucked it in the crook of his. "Why don't you tell me about Seth?" He began to walk, pulling her along, and she tried to protest but had no choice except to go with him.

Nick and Annie stood there in silence.

Finally, Nick broke it.

"How are you? Have you healed completely? You look lovely."

She absentmindedly patted her hair.

"Thank you. Yes, I'm perfectly well now."

"I'm glad to see you wearing the combs I gave you." He put his hand behind his back.

"Yes, I love them." She lowered her voice. "Evie misses you."

"I miss her."

"Then why do you stay away?" Her eyes filled with tears. "Because of me? Do I disgust you now?"

His mouth went slack at her words.

"No. Never." He took her hand in his. "I'm not good for you, or for Evie. Look at what's happened to you. You've been nearly stabbed, your hands were burned and you were shot—all of them my fault because I made you come work for me."

She cupped his jaw and looked up at him. "Nick, none of those things were your fault. You didn't make me come to work for you. I wanted to."

"No." He pulled away. "I made Blake give you the idea."

"I already had the idea before Blake even mentioned it. I needed a job and you gave me one. I would have done anything. If not for you, I'd have been a cleaning woman somewhere."

"Never, I'd—"

"You'd what? You did everything for me." She touched his arm again, rubbing up and down his bicep. "You kept me safer than I would have been anywhere else. Yes, things happened, but none were your fault. John Roland came to the saloon for Sarah and I'm glad I was there to help protect her. And I'm glad he's dead or she would have been. Of course, I'm not happy you were stabbed. You could have died. I would never have forgiven myself."

Recognizing the irony, he asked. "How would that have been your fault?"

She looked away. "I was taking care of you...I..."

He gently turned her head back to him and raised her chin with his knuckle. "You did everything you could for me, and I'm fine."

She nodded. "So am I. Walk with me. Please?"

She put her hand in the crook of his arm and they walked out of the simple, yet beautiful church, down the sidewalk toward the carriages parked on the street.

"Nick, I want to marry you. I know that I've been awful, all those times I turned you down, but please, marry me."

She felt him stiffen as they came to an abrupt halt.

He turned toward her, his eyes narrowed. "Why? Why now? Because you're rich? Because I'm not working in the saloon?"

She stopped and looked up into his beloved face. "None of that matters. I love you. Evie loves you and I don't care what my father thinks anymore. I want to be with you, see you every day, and make love to you every night. I don't know how much clearer I can make it."

He ran a finger along her jaw. "You truly don't care if your father doesn't give his blessing?"

"No. I don't believe as my father does any longer. I'm impressed and thankful to you for choosing to help me and reconciling with Seth. I'm glad you did it before he passed." She pulled back so she could look up into his face, see his expression.

"I don't know what to say."

"Say yes."

Nick took her in his arms and lowered his head to hers. "I love you, too," he whispered before his lips claimed hers.

His mouth slanted over hers and she wrapped her arms around his neck, returning his kiss. Putting all of her heart in the meeting of their lips.

"No!"

They heard a woman's scream and turned toward it.

Louisa ran at them and knocked them apart.

"No! He's mine," she screeched and leapt at Annie, sending her to the ground.

Annie fought back and hit Louisa in the face with her fist. "Get off me." Then she saw it. A small dagger flashed in Louisa's hand.

The deranged woman reared back and raised the dagger high. Just as she brought it down, Louisa was lifted off her and Annie was freed.

Nick held a kicking, screaming Louisa.

Blake helped up Annie from the ground. She brushed the grime from her skirt.

"After all I've done," Louisa shrieked, shaking her hair loose from its pins. "You would choose her over me? I got rid of Seth so we could be together. How could you do this to me?"

She yelled and squirmed, trying to get

away from Nick. Her hat hung to one side, her dress torn from rolling on the ground, and then she went limp in Nick's arms.

"It's ruined. It's all ruined because of her." She pointed at Annie and lunged out of Nick's grasp.

Annie raised her arm just as the dagger came down. It caught harmlessly in the strings of her reticule.

Nick grabbed Louisa again, forced her to drop the dagger, and this time held her in front of him with her arms pinned behind her back.

"Stop, Louisa. Be still!" he commanded. "What do you mean you got rid of Seth? Did you kill him?"

"Yes. For us." Tears streamed down her face. "I killed him for us."

Her eyes were wild. Insane. Annie had never seen anything like it before, and hoped to never see anything like it again.

"Blake, we need the police. We'll wait here while you go to get them," said Nick.

"Do you want to come with me, Annie?" asked Blake, nodding toward Louisa.

"No." Annie and Nick spoke simultaneously.

"I want Annie in my sight."

"I want to stay with Nick."

Blake nodded. "Are you sure?"

"We are," said Annie.

Louisa simply stared behind her at Nick, with a little smile on her face as she angled her head to rest on his shoulder. Annie knew then she'd lost all connection to reality.

Blake was also looking at Louisa. He lowered his gaze and shook his head, then he got in his carriage and went for the closest policeman.

"Take off my tie please, Annie," instructed Nick.

Annie cocked her head in question but did as he asked.

"Now bind her hands together, while I hold her arms."

He did as he said and Annie knotted the tie around the woman's wrists. The situation was safe now and Nick could let her go.

As soon as Nick released her she folded to the ground where she sat and hummed softly.

"What'll happen to her?" asked Annie.

"They'll put her in an insane asylum or in prison. I'll ask the judge for the asylum, though neither one will do her much good. I think her mind has snapped."

"I agree. Oh, Nick, what will happen to Frankie?"

"He'll go to an orphanage. Neither Louisa nor Seth had any other living relations. They were both only children and their parents died years ago."

Annie put her hand on Nick's arm. "We can't let that happen. None of this is his fault, he shouldn't be punished for it. That's what the orphanage would be for him. He's five. He'd live there until he's grown if we don't take him. Can't we take him in? Please? We could raise him as our son. I know Seth doted on the boy. He'd want this, Nick. You know he would."

Nick smiled down at her. "You amaze me sometimes. I totally agree. We'll have to go through the process to adopt him, but I don't think the courts will disagree. One less child in an orphanage will be all right with them. We'll go get him as soon as the police have collected Louisa. I'm glad she didn't bring him. I wouldn't have wanted him to witness this."

"Why didn't she bring him, do you suppose?"

"Honestly?"

"Of course."

"The way she was hanging on to me and with what she said, I think she intended to try to seduce me."

Annie nodded. "I think you're right." She looked at her toes, suddenly shy. "I think I should stay with you tonight...in case Frankie needs me."

"Look at me, sweetheart."

Excitement filled her as she looked up into the face of the man she loved.

"I want you to stay with me tonight, too. Not because Frankie might need you, but because I *do* need you. I know you want a big wedding, but can't we get married at the courthouse as soon as I can arrange it?"

Annie smiled wide. "Oh yes, please. I don't want to waste any more time apart."

"I know a judge who'll marry us tomorrow if I contact him. Is that too soon?"

"Absolutely not." Thrilled he didn't want to wait, her heart leapt. "Today would not be too soon. I can't wait to be Mrs. Nicholas Cartwright."

Nick took Annie in his arms and kissed her thoroughly. His lips drank from her, and she from him. She stood on her toes and wrapped her arms around his neck. She couldn't get close enough.

Breaking away for just a moment, she whispered, "Tonight is so far away. I can hardly wait."

"You little minx," he groaned. "I agree but wait we must." Nick set her from him as Louisa began to cackle and rock back and forth on the grass outside the church.

At the sound of carriages arriving, Annie and Nick turned to see Blake returning with the police. He approached with a policeman beside him.

"This is Captain Reynolds. I've told him everything that happened. He's here to collect Louisa."

"As you can see Captain, at this point, she has completely lost touch with reality," said Nick, gesturing toward the cooing woman.

"Please be gentle with her," added Annie, as the captain lifted Louisa to her feet.

"Yes, madam we'll take good care of her, but first I need to take her to headquarters and get the paperwork started for the murder investigation. Then the folks from the asylum will have to be notified, and they'll come get her."

Annie nodded. "I understand. Thank

you, sir."

They watched as Louisa was taken away.

"Will she be all right?" asked Annie.

"They'll do the best they can, but I have a feeling she won't know there is any other way," replied Nick.

He wrapped his arm around Annie's shoulders and pulled her close while they walked to his carriage.

"Where do you two think you're going?" said Blake with a knowing grin.

"Home," was all Nick said, and they kept walking.

"When should I tell Nellie the wedding is?" Blake called after them.

"Tomorrow," Nick called back.

Annie stopped. "We have to get Evie."

"Of course, I want her to be home as well. I want my family all together."

Blake smiled wide. "It's about darn time."

Annie knew she blushed, but she didn't care. Blake was right, it was about darn time. She'd wasted so much time, waiting for something she knew would never happen. Her irrational stance was her way of avoiding the situation. Putting it off on her father when in reality, she'd been scared. She'd just lost one husband and even though, she hadn't loved William, the fact remained he'd died married to her. What if something she'd done, or hadn't done, had caused his heart attack?

No! She wasn't responsible. William had worked himself into an early grave. That was all and as it turned out, he had given Annie her two greatest gifts. Evie and Nick.

Sad, she'd wasted so much time, she looked skyward. "Thank you, William," she said under her breath.

"What did you say?"

"Nothing important," Annie smiled up at her husband to be. The only man she could ever love. She wondered how she got so lucky.

They first went and picked up Evie.

As soon as she saw Nick, she ran to him as fast as her chubby legs would let her go.

"Dada, Dada," she hollered at the top of her lungs.

Nick beamed and scooped her into his arms.

"Hi, Sweet Pea. Miss me?" He kissed her forehead and she wrapped her arms around his neck and laid her head on his shoulder.

The look on Nick's face made Annie melt inside. She smiled. Her little family, and soon it would grow by one.

Nick was sure he could get a judge to perform the ceremony the next day, so Annie packed her emerald dress to get married in and, of course, she still wore the hair combs Nick gave her. Nellie loaned her the emerald necklace and ear bobs Blake had given her. They would look spectacular with the dress. Annie also packed enough clothes for Evie for a week, simply because she never knew if she would need more than one change of clothes. Evie was getting into everything now and keeping her clean was so hard.

After they got Evie, they drove to the Christenson residence to pickup Frankie. Nick had to explain the situation to the boy's nanny, Colleen. At first she didn't want to let him go but after hearing what had happened at the funeral, Colleen packed a valise for herself and one for Frankie. Seeing how close she was to Frankie, Nick thought having her in the household would be good, so he hired her on the spot, at double her current salary. After all, she could help with Evie, too.

Then Nick and Colleen went to talk to Frankie. Annie could tell it wasn't something he was looking forward to. How do you tell a five year-old that his mama is not coming home? Especially when he's just learned his papa is gone, too?

When she saw Nick enter the room with the boy, she spotted reddened eyes and wet cheeks. He wasn't really old enough to understand all that had happened, but he knew his parents weren't coming back and he'd be living with Nick and Annie. That was enough for now. When he was older, they would tell him the truth about his mother, before he heard it on the street.

Evie took to Frankie right away. She toddled over to him and took his hand. She was showing him that they would take care of him.

Annie's eyes filled with tears. Her baby girl was so smart. She looked up at Nick in time to see his eyes glistening. He bent and picked up them both.

"You are my children. That doesn't mean that we'll forget your father, Frankie. I honor him every day. I will take care of you until you're fully grown. I know it's a lot to take in right now, but when you're a little older, you'll understand all of this."

Blinking, Frankie nodded.

Evie grinned her one-toothed grin. "Dada" She laid her head on Nick's shoulder. Frankie, taking her cue, laid down his head, too.

The road ahead for Frankie would be long, but Annie and Nick willingly accepted it. They would keep his half of the company's proceeds safe until he was grown, along with the proceeds from the sale of all of his parent's property. They would pay for Louisa's stay at the asylum, but there was no way that she would ever be free again as long as she lived.

"Let's go home." Nick carried his children out of the Christenson house to the waiting carriage. He put down Frankie and the boy scrambled inside. Then Nick helped Annie in and handed her Evie before he entered himself.

The Christensen house was a few miles from Nick's as the crow flies, but up and down and around several hills as the roads were laid out. Even so the ride was fairly short.

Philip was waiting with the door open

by the time the coach came to a stop. "Do we have guests, sir?"

"No. We have family. Have Martha prepare the nursery for one Frankie Christensen, and Evie. She'll need to make a bed and a crib.

Nick looked down at the boy. "You'd like to stay with Evie tonight wouldn't you, Frankie? Or would you rather have your own room?"

"No, sir. I'd like to stay with Evie." He reached over and tickled Evie's leg.

The baby laughed.

She already seemed to love Frankie and he was certainly taken with her.

Annie thought they might become the best of friends.

CHAPTER 15

After giving instructions to Martha, Philip joined the family in Nick's library. "Would you care for dinner, sir? And would you like it served in here rather than the dining room?"

Philip was always one step ahead of Nick. That was why he'd hired the man. "Yes, we'll have dinner in here and make sure Cook prepares something the children will like."

"Yes, sir." He nodded and then hesitated. "Um, what would that be? None of us are familiar with having children in the house, sir. Well, except when you were injured, and Miss Evie was here. Mashed potatoes were the primary ingredient in her meals."

Annie chuckled.

"Have cook whip up some sandwiches with the leftover turkey. Do we have any milk? If not, then tea, and have her start getting milk delivered. The children will need it."

Nick turned to Annie. "You'll have to get together with Cook and have her stock the cupboards with the appropriate foods. I don't normally eat at home, as you know, and I have no idea what the staff eats."

She rolled her eyes and smiled. "They eat the same things we do."

After supper and some bedtime stories they put the children down for the night. Evie wanted to sleep with Frankie. She cried until finally, Nick moved her crib next to Frankie's bed. That seemed to appease her.

Frankie was happy to have her with him, too. Maybe when Annie was sure Evie wouldn't fall out of the bed, she'd let them sleep together. They comforted each other. Evie appeared glad to have a playmate and Frankie was glad to have someone his size rather than all the grown-ups.

"Are you ready?" Nick spoke the words softly against the side of Annie's neck as he wrapped his arms around her waist from behind.

Shivers ran down her spine straight to her toes. Ready? She was more than ready.

"Yes." She took his hand, led him out of the nursery, across and up the hall to his suite of rooms. "You don't mind if I stay in here with you? We could use the mistress's suite, if you'd rather."

"You're never leaving my bedroom again. You belong here, with me. We'll sleep here, love here, and make babies here."

She opened the door and suddenly Nick swept her up into his arms and carried her over the threshold. His room was lovely, done in dark oak so it was masculine but not so dark as to be dungeon-like. The posts at the corners of the foot-board were short, only about a foot high. The headboard was tall and had a rounded center with posts about three feet high at the corners. Two night stands and a desk were carved out of the same beautiful wood. In front of the fireplace were two overstuffed chairs upholstered in sky blue brocade, sitting on a magnificent Persian rug with indigo accents. Annie fell in love with the room when Nick was ill and needed frequent tending.

He walked across the room and set her down in the middle of the blue patchwork quilt that covered the bed.

"I love this quilt," said Annie. "But I'd love it more if you were here on it with me."

"My mother made it, and I intend to join you as soon as I take off some of these clothes."

Annie scooted to the edge of the bed. "Me, too. For what I have in mind, I definitely don't want to be wearing clothes."

Nick laughed. "Do you plan to seduce me, m'dear?"

"I don't need to seduce you, from the looks of it." She cocked an eyebrow and looked down at his trousers.

His full erection pressed against the front of his pants.

He shook his head. "I'm this way whenever I think of you. It's been awful, and somewhat embarrassing at times."

She stood and began unbuttoning her dress, starting with the satin rosette. "No more my darling. I'll be loving you enough, you won't need to miss me like you do now."

Annie dropped her bodice to the floor and undid the tapes at her waist that held her skirt. She let it, the slips and the crinoline underneath, slide to the floor on top of the bodice. Standing in her corset and pantaloons, heart racing, she crooked her finger at Nick.

"Come help me with my corset."

The corset unhooked in the front, so she didn't really need help, but she knew that once he was close enough, he wouldn't be able to keep his hands from her and she wanted them on her very much.

She wasn't wrong. Nick unhooked the corset quickly and replaced the material on her breasts with his hands.

"Your breasts are even more lovely than I imagined. Large enough to fill my hand to nearly overflowing, and your nipples." He lowered his head and took one in his mouth, suckling, and nipping at the hard little bud. "Are perfect for me."

Sheer joy ran through her as Annie threw back her head and held onto his shoulders. Her body tingled with delight and when he pulled away, she couldn't stop the little mew that came from the back of her throat.

Nick chuckled. "Like that do you, my love?"

"Oh, yes." The words were whispered on a sigh. "Very much."

He slid her pantaloons off her legs and she stood before him stark naked, in all ways, physically and emotionally.

"You have on too many clothes," Annie said, and began to unbutton his vest while he took off his jacket. Then he worked on his pants and she his shirt. Soon he was as nude as she was.

"You still amaze me," she said looking down. "And frighten me a bit, too."

"Don't be afraid. I won't hurt you, I promise. We'll be perfect together."

He pulled her close and kissed her. His tongue sought entry and she granted it.

They fed on each other, tasted, dueled and melted together.

Soon they were lying on the bed, each leaning up on one elbow, facing each other. Annie ran her hand up Nick's arm and he traced a line from her jaw, down her neck, between her breasts, circling under and around one breast, coming to rest on the nipple, which he pinched, lightly.

"Make love to me, Nick. I need you."

"Your demand is my wish."

He kissed her and rose over her,

positioning himself between her open legs, but rather than entering her as she desired, he scooted down and kissed her mons.

"Nick! What are you doing?" She tried to cover herself with her hands.

"Didn't William ever love you with his mouth?"

She shook her head. "No. Never."

"Then prepare to see heaven, my love."

He wasted no time and delved between her legs, finding her love bud and running his tongue over and around it.

"Nick! What are you doing to me?"

Every sensation in her body was centered in her groin. Her breath was hard to find and she panted her desire.

"Nick, please."

Everything in her welled up and she reached for the pinnacle, wanted to go over the edge, to the stars but couldn't. Then he scraped her bud with his teeth and she broke. She bucked and called his name. All the feelings she had for him came to the surface and she held his head in place. Then it was over and she released him.

He raised his head and grinned up at her.

"Did you like it?"

Still trying to control her breathing, she

gasped, "You know I did. You're ornery, Mr. Cartwright."

"I'm just getting started, my soon-to-be Mrs. Cartwright."

"I can't wait, Nick. I want to be married to you so much."

"We will be tomorrow, but tonight, we make love. We become man and wife in our hearts and minds and bodies."

She ran her fingers through his hair and pulled his head up to hers.

His long body covered her and their lips met once again.

"I'm going to make love to you. This is our beginning, Annie mine. 'Til the end of our days."

He rose over her and slid his member into her waiting sheath. She was slick with the love juices he'd already wrought from her. He stopped, pulled back and entered her a little farther. Then retreated.

"Nick," moaned Annie.

"I'm sorry, love."

She felt him begin to pull away and clamped her legs around his hips, preventing him from withdrawing.

"You misunderstand, darling. You're not hurting me. I simply need all of you. Now.

Don't go slow. Fill me, Nick. Love me."

He didn't answer with words, simply slid into her all the way to the hilt and began moving, pulling out of her and slamming back in over and over. Their bodies melded into one pulsing, aching, writhing body. They moved together as one, she pushing up as he pushed in, pulling back when he did. The movements, the ritual, were as old as time and yet for she and Nick, so new.

He pumped into her and her body tightened around him, he reached down and touched her, sent her off the edge and soaring to the sun. A faint shout she heard through her own moans told her Nick had reached the same place she had.

He collapsed upon her and she held him close, relishing the feel of his weight. Fully spent, just as she was. How long they stayed that way, she didn't know, just that she missed him when he rolled over.

He caught her about the waist and cuddled her into his side.

"I love you, Annie mine. Thank you for agreeing to marry me."

She reached up, cupped his jaw and ran her thumb back and forth, his whiskers abrasive to her soft skin. "I'm sorry I didn't accept your proposal sooner. So much time wasted."

He hugged her. "Everything happens for a reason, now we have Frankie and can protect him from his mother."

"You and I are together, and that's what really matters. We have Evie and Frankie and if we're very lucky we'll have made a baby tonight."

He grinned. "If not, we'll just keep trying. And if we did, we'll still keep trying."

Annie laughed. "Oh, you can count on that. I'm never letting you go, now that I have you.

Nick leaned down and kissed her. "You couldn't if you tried. You're stuck with me."

She grinned. "That's the kind of stuck I like."

Annie cozie'd up to Nick and closed her eyes.

"Oh no, you don't. Sleeping is not on the menu tonight. I intend to make love to you all night long."

"You can't, we're getting married tomorrow. We can't sleep in, even if Evie would let us."

"Try me." He slanted his mouth over

hers and built the fires within her again. Making love with Nick was everything she'd hoped it would be. He was gentle and fierce, the kind of man she'd always wished to find.

Happiness, like she'd never known before, welled up inside her.

*****

Annie sent word to her father and Doris that she was marrying and they were welcome to attend if they so chose. She didn't expect they would.

The judge, because he was a friend of Nick's and Blake's, came to Nick's house to marry them. He was the same one who had performed the ceremony for Nellie and Blake.

Annie shone in her emerald dress, her fiery red hair, loose down her back, the sides held back by the pearl combs.

Evie wore her best lavender dress with a white flounce at the bottom and sturdy little white walking shoes. Hair the color of flame, just like her mother's, formed ringlets around her head, with a purple ribbon that matched the trimming on her dress tied around some of the curls on top.

Frankie wore his best short pants that

Colleen had packed. She herself wore a dress, the color of a robin's egg. It looked spectacular with her coal black hair and blue eyes.

Nick was perfect in a charcoal gray suit with knee-length coat, matching vest and cravat, with a blue shirt. He'd slicked back his hair, but it curled just over his collar.

Annie couldn't stop herself from thinking about running her fingers through those curls. By the time the ceremony was over his hair would be dry and full of waves. He didn't like to use the oils and creams that most men did to keep their hair slicked down. Said it felt dirty and he'd been dirty enough in his life, he didn't need to make himself that way on purpose.

Sarah was present and would continue to live with them as long as she wanted. Annie had given her the dresses she'd worn while expecting. Sarah was showing now, her baby due in about two more months.

Philip and the rest of the staff attended, and had decorated the parlor with flowers from the garden. Bridget stayed up late baking cookies, and got up early to make luncheon for everyone to be served after the ceremony.

Annie looked over her family and friends gathered together to celebrate her marriage to Nick. She was so thankful for her life and where it had taken her.

The ceremony was short and simple. After Nick put a plain gold band on Annie's finger, the judge said, "I now pronounce you man and wife."

Nick kissed her long and hard, not at all the gentle peck she'd been expecting.

Blake and Nellie laughed. Evie laughed too because they were, and that made everyone else laugh.

"Congratulations, my friends," said Blake. He went to the side bar and opened the bottle of champagne he'd brought.

Philip brought champagne glasses for the adults and glasses of cider for Frankie and Evie. He was so thoughtful.

As they all, friends and staff alike, sat around the table for lunch, Nick stood. He took a spoon and gently tapped his water glass to get everyone's attention. "Thank you my friends, for being here with us today to share this special time. Our marriage was long in the making, and though there were times when it didn't look like it would happen, I had faith."

"You had faith, my boy?" said Hyrum from the door to the dining room. "I thought never to hear that phrase from you."

Nick walked over to his new father-in-law.

"Hyrum. Doris." He nodded to the woman who stood beside Annie's father. "I'm glad you decided to come. You've missed the ceremony."

"I apologize for that," said Hyrum. Dressed in his customary black he looked just like the preacher he was. "In all honesty, I couldn't decide whether I'd be welcome or not. I hope you don't mind us letting ourselves in."

"Not at all, you're my wife's father, you'll always be welcome. I would never come between you and her." He held out his hand.

Hyrum shook Nick's offered hand.. "I heard about how you saved her life again. I'm grateful for that. She does seem to get herself into trouble. I'm glad you've been there to save her."

"I'll always be here for everyone I care about. Please, come in," Nick waved toward the table. "There's plenty of food and champagne." He looked at his father-in-law and cocked an eyebrow. "Or cider, if you prefer."

"Actually," said Doris, "I'd really like to see our granddaughter. I've never had children of my own, and would like to get to know you and yours." She was the opposite of her husband, dressed in a canary yellow walking dress, with matching hat. The look was almost overly bright, but with her dark brown hair, only now beginning to streak with gray, the effect was striking.

Annie walked over to them, carrying Evie and holding Frankie's hand.

"Father, you know Evie and this is Frankie." She looked down at the boy. "This is your Grandfather and Grandmother Markum."

"Ma'am. Sir," said Frankie

Doris knelt down to Frankie's level, "Hello, Frankie. I'm very happy to meet you and, when you're ready, I'd love to be your Grandma Doris." She held out her hand.

He shook it.

"Yes, ma'am, Grandma Doris. I never had no grandparents before."

Doris looked up at Annie, tears in her eyes.

"Well I've never had a grandson before

either. We can learn together."

"Yes, Gran...Grandma Doris, I'd like that."

Evie kicked and wanted down, so Annie set her on the floor. She walked over to Doris and patted her cheek.

The tears in Doris' eyes ran down her cheeks and she grinned in spite of them. "Hello, Evie. Can you say Grandma?"

"Mama," Evie looked and pointed at Annie.

"Yes, you sweet thing, that's Mama. We'll have to work on Grandma."

Annie's father looked down on the exchange. She saw the tears in his eyes and knew her children had won him over, where she could not. She picked up Evie and walked with her to him.

"Do you remember Grandfather Hyrum?" she asked to her baby girl.

Evie cocked her head to the side and gazed at the man, then popped her finger in her mouth and laid her head on her mother's shoulder.

"Hello, Evie," said Hyrum.

His deep voice rumbling over Annie. She sometimes forgot that his voice, even when not delivering a sermon, was impressive.

Hyrum reached out his hand and ran a finger down Evie's arm.

She giggled.

He looked up at Annie, a grin spread across his face. "You were always ticklish as a baby."

He ran his finger along Evie's arm again and she giggled again. Then he held his arms out to her.

She looked at him a minute before leaning away from her mother and going to him.

Tears ran down Hyrum's cheeks, but there was a wide grin on his face.

He looked at Nick. "Thank you for ignoring an old man too set in his ways, and marrying my little girl. You've made her happy, this I can see, and isn't that all any parent wants for his child? To be happy. And in Annie's case, to be safe."

"Yes, sir. Now that she'll be remaining home—"

"Only until I open my café."

Nick looked skyward and groaned. "You're still doing that?"

"Yes, all those people down by The Nugget need a place to go for food that is quiet and just about the food. Not all of them go there for the…other reasons. Some just want a meal."

"All right. Whatever you want to do."

Annie beamed. "I knew you'd help me."

"I'll do anything for you," Nick wrapped his arm around her shoulders and brought her to his side.

"I know." She pulled him down for a kiss right there in front of everyone, and she didn't give a fig what her father thought.

CHAPTER 16

Everyone filled their plates with the roast beef, ham, Duchess Potatoes, asparagus spears, and for dessert, Bridget had managed to make a cake. A yellow cake with white boiled icing covered in flaky coconut. It was delicious and Annie told Bridget she wanted it at least once a year on the anniversary of her and Nick's marriage.

Bridget blushed, unused to the praise, but said, "Of course, madam, I'll add it to my calendar."

Nick looked around the table. Hyrum and Doris joined them at the table and talked to Evie, who sat in Hyrum's lap, much to his delight. Everyone else was talking and laughing, enjoying the day.

"A penny for your thoughts," said

Annie, while she ran her stocking'd foot up his pants leg.

He leaned over, so they couldn't be heard, "I'm happy to have such a wonderful family and such a beautiful wife."

Annie blushed. He loved making her blush and it was so easy to do.

Blake suddenly laughed. "I don't know what you two are talking about, but I can guess. Nellie and I have been talking and we'd like to watch the children while you two take a little trip for your honeymoon."

Nick looked at Annie, who simply smiled.

He looked back at Blake and Nellie. "Thank you but no thank you. Annie and I have waited so long to be a family, we don't want to miss another minute of us all being together."

Blake nodded. "I totally understand my friends. Even though Nellie and I didn't have to wait, it's been marvelous to have my family."

"I understand you'll be growing by one. Perhaps you and Nellie should leave the kids with us, and you two take a little trip. Or even go to a hotel for a week and you simply show Nellie the city," Nick bent toward

Blake so only he could hear. "Or stay in bed for a week, no children to get you up or need feeding or…anything."

Nick leaned back and took Annie's hand, brought it to his lips and kissed it. "Although that thought, definitely sounds intriguing."

Annie shook her head. "As wonderful as being alone with you sounds, I know Frankie has been through enough without his parents disappearing again, even for just a week." She looked over at Blake and Nellie. "We'd love to keep your children for a few weeks. It would be wonderful for Frankie to have another boy to play with and he and Henry seem to be getting along well." She nodded her head in the direction of the boys who sat next to each other deep in conversation.

"What do you think, Blake? Could we?" asked Nellie, her eyes lit up.

"Your family is expanding, you better take us up on the offer before you have too many more children," teased Nick.

"Where would we go?" asked Blake of Nellie.

"Just a short trip to a hotel, the nicest one in town, then you will do nothing but show me the sights of San Francisco and surrounding countryside for two weeks. I want to visit everything, every one of your favorite restaurants. I want to visit a winery, and see if they will show us how wine is made, I—"

"All right, all right, I get the idea." He turned toward Nick and Annie. "We'll be taking you up on your offer, but not right away. You need time together to get settled in to being married."

Nick sat at the head of the table with Annie to his right. Blake sat across from her. The table held twenty people and even with all their family, friends and staff, room remained for seven more to sit. Annie thought if Nick had his way they'd fill up the table with children. She wanted more but only a few, not seven. Goodness sakes, just the thought of birthing seven more children made her flush and she had to fan herself.

Nick noticed the movement. "What are you thinking?"

"That there are still seven chairs at this table and I refuse to fill them all with children."

Nick laughed. "We don't have to birth the children to have more. We included

Frankie in our family. I bet there are lots of children at the orphanage that would love to have a home."

Annie placed her hand in Nick's and squeezed. "Oh, Nick, do you think we could? I do want a big family but the thought of birthing that many children is daunting, to say the least."

"We'll talk more about it later, but I don't see why not."

Annie's dreams were all coming true. There would be more children, Frankie and Evie would have lots of brothers and sisters. And she had Nick, her wonderful, handsome, generous, funny husband. He was her secret wish and so much more. He was all her dreams wrapped into one.

Evie stood in Hyrum's lap.

The man seemed to have no control over his granddaughter but he was grinning.

"Mama! Dada!" she hollered over the din of voices at the table.

Annie and Nick both looked and so did everyone else. Suddenly all was quiet and Evie had the floor.

"Papa," she said, and patted Hyrum's cheeks. She looked over at Doris, "Gama." She pointed at her grandmother.

Doris burst into tears. "I'm very happy to be your Gama," she told Evie.

"Hahee," said Evie, and she sat down and put her thumb into her mouth.

"I think that about says it all," said Nick as he leaned close. "Happy. Are you happy, my love?"

"Oh yes, more than I ever thought I would be."

"Me, too, because you're in my life. Thank you for making me the happiest man in the world, by marrying me and giving me the family I didn't know I longed for."

"Thank you, my love, for waiting for me."

"Always.

EPILOGUE

Christmas, 1872

Annie entered the parlor where they had set up the Christmas tree. Heavily pregnant with their sixth child, she wore her dressing gown because nothing else seemed to fit tonight.

Frankie was amazing. Now eight, he was so good with the other children. He kept them in line without seeming like a bossy, older brother. The little ones looked up to him.

Through correspondence,, Nick and Annie kept tabs on Louisa. They would tell Frankie about his mother when he was older. For now, he needed to just be a child. The doctors said she hadn't regained any of her sanity and probably never would.

Evie, now three, had been joined by Seth nine months after Annie and Nick got married. He was not yet two and into everything with Evie leading the way. He looked just like Nick with golden brown hair and brown eyes that sparkled with mischief.

Annie hoped she had another girl this time. That event would keep them even. Three boys and three girls. But in reality she didn't care what they had as long as it was a healthy baby. She'd been lucky with the others, and they were all thriving.

True to his word, she and Nick adopted a brother and sister from the orphanage. Margaret, four, and Gregory, six. Both children had coal black hair and vibrant blue eyes. Their parents had died in an accident and they were sent to the orphanage. Reverend Schossow, who ran the orphanage, was there when they'd come in. They were already too old for adoption by most people and the reverend wanted to keep them together, so he got in touch with Nick. The children had only been with Nick and Annie for about six months, but they'd come to love them as much as they did any of the other children.

She and Nick definitely had a houseful, and they loved it.

Nick looked up from his chair by the fire. He was reading *'Twas The Night Before Christmas* to the children. They were all having hot chocolate, and Evie sat in his lap as she always did when he was around.

Annie knew that a mother shouldn't have favorites when the subject was her children, but Evie was the one, in a way, who had brought them all together. Her birth reintroduced Nick back into her life, and so had started their family.

Evie and Nick had a special bond. She was his baby girl, his sweet pea and always would be. Annie didn't want to think about what any young man who wanted to court Evie would have to go through when meeting her father. Nick would not make the situation easy on anyone who wanted to marry his daughter.

The circumstance was funny in a way. Annie remembered her father hadn't wanted her to marry Nick, and though they were not the best of friends, they did get along now. Of course, the fact that her father and Doris had been gone for the first two years of Nick and Annie's marriage, and had only been back for a short time, might have had something to do with it.

Annie walked into the room and started for the chair beside Nick's in front of the fire. She hadn't gone three steps before she stopped again with a gasp. The warm liquid flowing down her leg told her the night would be a long one. She'd been having labor pains for hours. Little ones. Far apart but getting closer and she didn't want to say anything because she didn't want to spoil the day.

"Ah, Nick?"

"Yes, sweetheart?" He looked up from the book. "Are you ready to join us for our story?"

"I'd love to, but I think we'll be having a baby tonight."

"We have five babies tonight who are ready for Santa...oh! You mean that baby." He set Evie on the floor and fairly leapt from the chair.

"I guess it's a good thing that Nellie and Blake are coming for Christmas. They should be here soon."

He scooped Annie into his arms and she wrapped hers around his neck. His hair was a little too long, as usual, and curled over his collar. She ran her fingers through it, then laid her head on his shoulder.

"Children," he said over his shoulder. "Don't get into any trouble. Frankie, go tell Philip to send for the doctor. We're having a baby."

"Yes, Papa."

Frankie ran off in the direction of the kitchen.

Annie knew Bridget would soon be out with more hot chocolate and cookies and Colleen would finish reading the story to keep the children occupied.

"Are you ready to be a father again?" she asked softly. She knew what the answer would be, but never tired of hearing it.

"Always. We can never have too many children."

"I don't know about that. We'll have six with this one."

"And we still have two more bedrooms to fill after he or she gets here. There are lots of children out there who need our love. For now though, we'll stop for a while with six."

She smiled. He always knew what to say to make her happy. "What shall we name this one?"

He carried her up the stairs and to the

mistress's chamber. It was their birthing room and nursery when the babies were little. Annie didn't have as far to go to nurse them that way. Of course, when they were newborn, they had a bassinette in the master bedroom. Seth had stayed there until he was about two months old. Then they moved him to the mistress's suite and a crib. Now he was in the nursery with Evie and Margaret.

"I don't know. What do you think?"

"I like Christina if it's a girl, especially if she's born tonight. Christmas night."

"And if it's a boy?"

"I was thinking of Jonathan. What do you think?"

"You know I love whatever names you come up with."

He entered the bedroom and set down Annie.

"Good thing you are only wearing your night dress and dressing gown."

"Nothing else fits."

"I think you were just thinking ahead. Now let me help you out of them and into a dry nightgown."

He deftly stripped her of both garments and put on the one she'd laid out on the bed. "I see you had already planned for this," he said looking at the clean nightgown.

"I thought the birth might happen. I like to be prepared."

He slipped the nightdress over her head and arms then let it fall nearly to the floor. Then he turned down the bed, scooped her up and set her in the middle.

"I could get into bed by myself," she admonished.

"And strain yourself before you have to? I don't think so. Besides, doing so lets me prove that I'm still the strong, handsome man you married."

She cupped his cheek. "You will always be that man. Even when we're eighty years old."

"Ha! Then the kids will be taking care of us."

"Maybe," she agreed. "Lie with me for a while."

"I'd like nothing better."

He climbed into the bed beside her, put her head on his shoulder, and cuddled her to his side.

"Thank you for saving me, Annie," he whispered. "For giving me the wonderful life we have."

She brought his hand to her lips and

kissed it. "I think we saved each other, my love. I couldn't have survived with any happiness without you and who knows how Evie would have turned out." She took a deep breath.

"Does it hurt badly?"

"Only for a short time. The doctor better get here soon though, or you'll be delivering this baby."

"Now we can't have that," said a deep voice from the doorway.

Nick popped up to greet the man. "Doctor Walsh. Glad you could make it so quickly."

"It's Christmas, my boy. Was home with the family. Philip knew where to find me. Now, Nick, you know what to do. Send Martha with towels and hot water. I want to wash up before I deliver this little mite."

"Yes, sir."

Nick left the room at a good clip.

"You only do that so you can get him out of the room," said Annie.

"Not true, my dear. I do wash before I deliver but I also make sure I do it before I get here, in case the baby is in a hurry. Now let's see where we're at."

He lifted Annie's gown and spread her

knees.

"Looks like this one is not waiting much longer. It's already crowning."

"I know," Annie groaned as a pain sliced across her big belly.

"You can holler if you want, Annie. I don't mind."

"Well, I do. I don't want to scare the children. Oww."

"Understood."

Martha came in with the water and towels.

Nick was hot on her heels.

"Thank you, Martha. Nick the baby is coming, you should probably leave now."

"All right, Doc." He went to Annie and gave her a quick kiss. "I love you."

She took a deep breath and groaned. Then breathed hard after a moment. "I love you, too. Now go be with the children. They'll worry."

"I'm going now." He bent down and kissed her again this time on the forehead. "See you shortly."

"I'm afraid you're right about that. Now go."

Annie watched his retreating form and then let out the moan she'd been holding.

"I want you to push now, Annie," the doctor said.

"Yes, push. I want to push."

She bore down as hard as she could. Then stopped and rested. They went through that bearing down and resting for twenty minutes.

Finally, the doctor said, "this is the one, now push, push for all you're worth Annie. Push."

She did and felt the babe slide from her body. Then she heard a slap and a small cry.

"What is it?"

"A baby boy. A beautiful, red-haired baby boy. Martha, you get him cleaned up and then tell Nick. I'll finish here."

Annie nodded, too tired to say anything. A few minutes later, Martha handed her the baby and she wasn't so tired any more. He was red-faced and screaming. He had a great pair of lungs.

Nick ran into the room. "I heard the baby. What is it?"

"We have another son. Come see."

Grinning, Nick walked to the bed and looked down on his new son. "He looks like his mother."

"Just the hair. He has your nose," teased

Annie. "But he's a hungry boy." She opened her nightgown and held the baby to her breast.

With a little encouragement, he latched on to her nipple and began to suckle.

"He's beautiful. Thank you for my new son." Nick bent down and kissed Annie softly, and then kissed the baby.

"Let him finish nursing before you get the other children," said Annie.

"And the rest of the family. Blake and Nellie and their brood are here. Sarah, James and Jenny are here as well."

"Good. I'm so glad that Sarah married James. He's a good, kind man. He'll treat her and Jenny right."

"Since all of our family and friends are here, we'll celebrate Christmas and Jonathan's arrival," said Nick. "I'll bring you supper later, but first I want to give you your Christmas present. You've already given me mine." He rubbed the little head of his newborn son.

The baby wrinkled his nose but kept nursing.

"What did you get me?" She was suddenly excited. With the birth of her son, she'd forgotten that it was still Christmas.

"Open it, you'll see."

Annie took the box from him and opened it. Inside was a beautiful gold ring with a sparkling blue sapphire surrounded with dazzling diamonds.

"I never gave you the ring I wanted to when we got married. I want to give it to you now."

"Oh, Nick. It's beautiful."

He took her hand and, before he put it on next to the plain gold band she wore, he asked, "Will you marry me, Annie Markum White? To live with me all of our days?"

Annie smiled and cupped his face with her hand. "I will marry you. Always. I love you, Nick."

"And I love you, Annie mine."

THE END

ABOUT THE AUTHOR

Cynthia Woolf is the award winning and best-selling author of ten historical western romance books and two short stories with more books on the way. She was born in Denver, Colorado and raised in the mountains west of Golden. She spent her early years running wild around the mountain side with her friends.

Their closest neighbor was one quarter of a mile away, so her little brother was her playmate and her best friend. That fierce friendship lasted until his death in 2006.

Cynthia is an avid reader. Her mother was a librarian and brought new books home each week. This is where young Cynthia first got the storytelling bug. She wrote her first story at the age of ten. A romance about a little boy she liked at the time.

Cynthia loves writing and reading romance. Her first western romance Tame A Wild Heart, was inspired by the story her mother told her of meeting Cynthia's father on a ranch in Creede, Colorado. Although Tame A Wild Heart takes place in Creede that is the only similarity between the stories. Her father was a cowboy not a bounty hunter and her mother was a nursemaid (called a nanny now) not the ranch owner.

Cynthia credits her wonderfully supportive husband Jim and the great friends she's made at CRW for saving her sanity and allowing her to explore her creativity.

TITLES AVAILABLE

NELLIE – The Brides of San Francisco 1
ANNIE – The Brides of San Francisco 2
REDEEMED BY A REBEL (Book 1, Destiny in Deadwood series)
HEALED BY A HEART (Book 2, Destiny in Deadwood series)
SEDUCED BY A SINNER (Book 3, Destiny in Deadwood series)
CAPITAL BRIDE (Book 1, Matchmaker & Co. series)
HEIRESS BRIDE (Book 2, Matchmaker & Co. series)
FIERY BRIDE (Book 3, Matchmaker & Co. series)
TAME A WILD HEART (Book 1, Tame series)
TAME A WILD WIND (Book 2, Tame series)
TAME A WILD BRIDE (Book 3, Tame series)
TAME A SUMMER HEART (short story, Tame series)
TAME A HONEYMOON HEART (short story in the Lost In A Kiss Anthology)

WEBSITE – www.cynthiawoolf.com
NEWSLETTER - http://bit.ly/1qBWhFQ